Her Brand of Trouble

By

ALYSIA S. KNIGHT

Heart Dreams
PRESS

Her Brand of Trouble
By Alysia S. Knight
Published by Heart Dreams Press
Copyright © 2015 Alysia S. Knight
Cover design: by Kelli Ann Morgan @
www.inspirecreativeservices.com

ISBN:1942000111
ISBN-13:978-1-942000-11-2

Also available from Alysia S. Knight

Letting Love Win

☙

Past To Die For

☙

Temperature Rising

☙

Kare for Me

☙

Blind Witness

☙

Beauty and the Chief

☙

Trail to Her Heart

☙

His Governess

☙

The Ruin - Out of Time

I hope you enjoy.

Best Wishes,

Alysia S. Knight

Chapter One

"Now, Rachael, aren't you glad you came?"

Rachael Jacobs swung her attention from the country band on the stage, over the dance floor and around the room. "It's still so flashy."

"It's Vegas. It's supposed to be flashy. Lighten up."

Rachael studied the dance floor as if thinking of it for a picture. People crowded the place. Men dressed in cowboy hats, jeans and boots. Women wore a wide array of fashions, from full swirling skirts to skin tight ones, designer jeans to ragged shorts. They all swirled on the wooden dance floor. People two-stepped and swayed to the music that filled the room, almost drowning out the conversations of her fellow photographers gathered around the table.

"I'm glad." She smiled truly happy she'd let Mary talk her into coming. The perky, petite, forty-five year old redhead was good at talking her into things. That's how she ended up being scheduled to speak at the photography convention the next day. The brief thought of the conference lecture sent a wave of terror through her.

Rachael liked life behind the camera. Preferably in the woods, anywhere that was not in front of a crowd, though the benefits of a national award were exciting. The opportunity it brought was still mind-boggling.

For several minutes Rachael watched the dancers and band while trying to calm her racing heart. The waitress drew her attention for an order. "A root beer, please, if you have it?" When the waitress nodded, Rachael turned back toward the stage.

"Now, that is a man worth photographing." Mary's comment caught Rachael's attention, and she followed the direction of Mary's gaze.

Rachael caught sight of the man who'd just stepped through the doorway and felt her insides lurch. His attire proclaimed him a cowboy and something in his stance and the muscles that filled the chambray shirt and Levi's affirmed it.

Rachael's breath caught as her eyes met his from across the room. His gaze seemed to reach her soul and it was as if she'd never be the same again.

"He's worth a lot more than taking pictures of." Chantell's saccharine sweet voice brought Rachael's head around, breaking eye contact from the man to look at the woman on the other side of the table. Chantell Willis stood, pressed her red coated lips together, smoothed the short, tight skirt over her hips and, with a toss of her head, headed for the man.

Rachel could only watch, knowing she could never pull off that walk. They might be in the same league in wildlife photography, but she was no competition to Chantell when it came to men. Chantell didn't even hesitate approaching the handsome cowboy, who hadn't even had a chance to put in his order before she staked her claim. He seemed to hesitate only slightly before, to Rachael's horror, he followed Chantell to their table.

Cஜண

Brand Morgan still hadn't got his heart to beat normal since his eyes came in contact with the woman seated at the table across the room. It was the first time he'd ever had his breath knocked out of him just by looking at a woman. And, he couldn't even see much of her sitting at the table.

She wasn't overly gorgeous, but pretty—yes. The wheat-colored hair, that he figured didn't come from a bottle, was long, though at the moment it was pulled up in some kind of twist, leaving her trim neck bare. He couldn't make out the color of her eyes, but they were striking.

He didn't register the other woman who rose from the table until she was right in his face. The woman was gloss and show, beautiful and dressed in a way that didn't hide much of her considerable attributes. She left him cold, but with a glance to the table she came from, he accepted her invitation to join them.

Two men and three women sat around the table. A sassy, middle-aged redhead was the first to greet him though he had trouble concentrating on what she said when another jolt hit him as he caught a shy glance from the woman beside her.

Blue eyes, she had blue eyes the color of a clear summer day. They tilted away from him when the ebony haired Chantell wrapped her highly polished finger tips around his arm.

"This is Brand." The red crested lips cooed.

"Nice to meet you, Brand. I'm Mary," the redhead introduced the others at the table. Brand managed to nod in acknowledgment until she got to the woman next to her, "and this is Rachael."

The woman's eyes came up to his when her name was announced. Her lips parted in a tiny O, drawing his gaze to them with a quickening of his heartbeat again. He wondered if she felt any of the stirring he was feeling.

"Where are you from?" Mary asked as he sat down.

"Arizona."

"Here on vacation?" the woman continued.

"Not really." His answer was interrupted by the waitress bringing the drinks and turned to take his order. "Cola, please," he asked without hesitation.

"Oh, you can order something stronger. We already have a designated driver. Rachael doesn't drink." Chantell made it sound like a nasty secret.

"Actually, I'm not much of a drinker myself," he commented easily as he turned to answer Mary's question. "I'm here to pick up a couple horses."

"Oh, so you're a real cowboy," Chantell gushed.

ᘓᘔ

Rachael had to fight to keep from rolling her eyes. She wasn't sure which of the woman's moods was worse—the simpering flirt or nasty competitor, which Rachael had quite a bit of first-hand experience with.

Rachael took another quick glance at the handsome cowboy and knew the only place for him would be in her dreams.

Chapter Two

Her dreams had never been like this before. They had never made her feel so content and full of love. Light filtered through the crack in the curtain, pulling Rachael toward awareness. She fought it, pressing her face into the warm, hard chest, breathing in the musky smell which encircled her. The hand that stroked up and down her back was rough and callused, like the other hand that pressed her possessively close.

It was the tickling of hair on her nose that brought her to the last step of awareness. Her eyes flew open the instant her hand registered the matted hair and warm skin. She was greeted with a view of tanned skin, and dark hair, both of which covered totally masculine muscles.

Raising her head slightly, her eyes slid over a prominent Adam's apple to the whisker-shadowed jaw, and the face right out of her dreams. The startled sound that escaped her throat brought a stirring next to her. A bare muscular leg brushed against her smooth one.

As Rachael shifted, it brought another response from the man. His hand tightened on her waist, and his face turned down to brush his lips against her forehead. Rachael couldn't keep her eyes from closing for an instant in pleasure, before forcing them back open. She looked right into misty gray-green eyes.

Dreamy confusion flooded her a moment before reality hit. And for the first time, she realized the man in her bed was real, not her dream. A cry broke from her as she jumped back. Another followed as the sheet dropped. She squeaked again grabbing the sheet, pulling it to her.

"Rachael?" The deep male voice sounded sleepy and confused. The hand that reached for her was non-threatening but did nothing to ease her panic.

"No!" Rachael cried, stumbling out of bed, dragging the blankets with her.

Color swept through her face before she turned and fled to the bathroom. Her first hint she wasn't in her own room was when the bathroom wasn't where it should have been. The next hint was the unfamiliar shaving kit by the sink instead of her small makeup bag.

Confusion swamped her body, as she deflated back against the door she had slammed behind her. Rachael sank to the floor unable to stop the tears cascading down her face.

What had she done?

ೞೋ

Brand wasn't quite sure what was happening, but it was clear enough the woman he'd been making love to in his dreams had been as real as the totally satiated feeling that said he had had the most incredible night of his life.

He stumbled from the bed and shook his head to clear the unnerving fogginess which lingered. Luckily, his hotel room had an additional vanity outside the bathroom. The cold water he splashed on his face helped clear his mind.

He could hear the sobs from the woman on the other side of the door. It'd been a long, long time since he'd experienced any morning-afters, and none had ever been like this.

From the fog, he conjured up the details of the night before. He remembered clearly going to listen to the country band, wanting to relax and unwind after the long drive. He remembered the first sight of Rachael across the room and the long absent desire which filled his chest.

It had taken some maneuvering once at the table to get away from the raven-haired shark who had invited him there. Then he'd invited Rachael Jacobs, wildlife photographer from a small town in Wyoming, to dance and the evening became a dream.

His heart raced at the thought of her in his arms, but it wasn't just the chemistry that flowed between them. It was the way he found himself talking to her about everything. First were the safe subjects—wildlife, horses, then on to family, hopes, dreams and life.

Rachael's associates were totally forgotten, and when the group announced they were headed to another bar, Rachael declined saying it was time for her to end the night and get some sleep. As he held her in his arms for one last dance, he hadn't wanted the night to end, but knew it had to. He wasn't into one-night stands and knew instinctively Rachael wasn't either.

Back at the table, while they finished their drinks, he gave her his address and phone number, hoping she might call and they might be able to continue the relationship he felt starting. That was when things began to get cloudy.

He did remember asking to see her safely to her room, and after some persuading, she agreed. On the way out a song started which caught her attention and when she told him it was one of her favorites, he'd seen it as an opportunity to hold her in his arms for one last dance. Moments of the dance were blurry.

Shaking his head, he remembered the feel and heat of her body as she swayed against his. He remembered the blinding desire to taste her, when he asked her for a kiss he was surprised when her lips met his in an unschooled timid way that swamped his heart.

The sob from the other side of the door pulled him from his reverie. "Rachael?" He tapped on the door. "Rachael, sweetheart." The endearment came out easily, but no answer returned. "Rachael, come out."

He could hear the sobs clearly as she tried to stop crying. "Rachael, open the door."

"I ... I can't."

He heard the quiet voice. "Yes, you can." Then noticing himself in the mirror, he grabbed his jeans and pulled them on. "Rachael, come out so we can talk."

"I don't ... I've never." The sobs picked up and so did something else in his mind. The kisses and desires had grown on the dance floor until it was almost unbearable. He said truthfully, he wasn't into casual sex, but he'd wanted her. Her words hit him hard, when she said she'd never.

His eyes shot to the bed. Even in his fogged mind, he remembered she'd been a virgin. All innocent and giving to him the gift she was saving for her husband.

Him!

His eyes shot to the scrolled paper on the dresser. Without opening it, he knew what it said. *The Marriage of Brand Justin Morgan to Rachael Ann Jacobs.* They'd signed it right after the minster of the little chapel not far from the hotel announced them husband and wife. It had been all he could take to wait to get Rachael up to his room to make her his.

Resting his elbows on the counter, he pushed his hands through his hair. Trying to think clearly, if he was a drinking man he'd say he was drunk, but he'd given up alcohol when he turned twenty-two. The last eight years he'd been dry.

Though little made sense, he decided his first concern was Rachael. Her cries had softened. "Rachael." He kept his voice gentle. "Sweetheart, it's Brand." *Stupid, she knew who he it was.* "It's all right."

"No." The word was a whisper.

"Yes."

"I ... I," she stuttered. Not getting anything else out, but at least she was talking.

"Rachael, I want you to remember last night." The sob he heard reached his breaking point. "Rachael, I'm coming in." Putting his shoulder to the door, he pushed.

"No!" she squeaked. "I don't have any clothes on."

"Wrap the blanket around you then, because I'm coming in." He felt the resistance of her body against the door, but as he continued to press, it moved away. The woman huddled in the sheet on the floor looked up with a tear-streaked face that showed as much confusion as he felt, mixed with a heavy dose of fear.

It probably wasn't the best idea, but he couldn't stop himself. "Oh, Rachael." Dropping to his knees, he pulled her into his arms. Her body stiffened, but he didn't let that stop him from holding her. It was a full minute before she relaxed against his chest, and he felt his skin go wet with tears that burned to his soul.

Tucking her tight under his chin, his heart nearly burst when he felt one quivering hand snake around his neck. Sliding an arm underneath her, he gathered her close and stood. A small gasp accompanied the other arm shooting around him.

"Easy," he whispered into her hair. Surprisingly enough she relaxed against him. It took him only a couple steps to reach the end of the bed, where he settled with her in his lap.

Rachael looked up in alarm but didn't pull back. Brand couldn't keep the smile from his face. The sheet was wrapped tightly around her, but it still revealed the soft, smooth skin of her shoulders. It was her face looking up to him so full of innocence that caused him to rein in his thoughts.

"Do you remember what happened last night?"

Her body tensed immediately.

He laid his finger on her lips. "I'm not talking about making love. I'm talking about before."

"At the ... at the," she started again, "bar. I shouldn't have gone. I don't even drink. I shouldn't ...."

Brand stopped her with his finger back against her lips. "Shh, I'm talking after that, but before we got to my room." He pointed to the paper scroll then lifted her left hand to display the ring on her finger that sported a large diamond.

Confusion was strong on her face.

"Rachael, that paper says we're married." Saying the words for the first time aloud hit him hard in the stomach.

The way Rachael's eyes dilated attested that it didn't hit her any better. The next instant she fled his lap. He didn't even have time to react before he heard her being sick in the bathroom.

He had never given much serious thought to getting married, but he didn't think the thought of being married to him was enough to make a woman sick. Heck, he even had quite a few women chasing him. Getting off the bed, he started for the bathroom then stopped, unsure how she would handle his invasion of her privacy. Pacing back and forth at the end of the bed, he'd never felt more at a loss.

Brand paused on his seventh lap across the room, his eyes rested on the scroll. An odd feeling of calmness came over him as he reached out, picked it up and slid the ribbon from it, reading the words proclaiming their marriage.

CBEO

Rachael's stomach finally settled enough she dared stand. Her legs threatened to give way. She made it to the sink. The cold water did little to wash the confusion from her mind or taste from her mouth.

Everything seemed scattered in pieces and the biggest one was the man on the other side of the door. She tried to pull it all together in her mind, but it was so jumbled up. The only thing she knew for certain, though she didn't understand why, was she felt cared for.

She remembered the first moment she saw Brand. He was so incredible. She was surprised when he paid attention to her instead of Chantell, who didn't bother hiding what she was offering. Even more surprising was the comfortable way she felt with him. Things didn't get foggy until the evening was most of the way over. Until then, it had been like a crystal clear dream.

He'd asked her to dance. And when he had taken her into his arms, they had talked, really talked. He'd been surprisingly easy to talk to. She wished she knew what to say now.

She splashed water on her face again looking in the mirror, she was still pale. *So much for how she was handling the first time ever awaking with a man.* She suppressed a groan.

She tried to make herself feel better about the oddities of the situation, but they were way above what she was prepared for. Staring down at the ring on her finger, she couldn't believe it. She was married. Okay, that was terrifying.

"Oh," she groaned. How many women get sick the first thing? Rachael pressed her face into her hands. Pulling herself up, she splashed more water on her face before forcing herself to go greet the man who was her husband.

Brand stood in the middle of the room. The scroll in his hand held his entire attention. She couldn't see what he was thinking, but she guessed, since this was as unexpected for him as it was for her, his thoughts were probably on how to get out of it.

"Brand." Her voice cracked, but this time she was in more control of herself.

His head came up, and he took a step toward her and then stopped. She didn't know him well enough to read his expressions, but concern was highly visible.

"Are you all right?" His voice was low, soft, a touch hesitant. It seemed a bit strange coming from the big, strong, confident man of the night before.

"Yes." She tried to smile reassuringly but knew it came out weak and glanced away embarrassed.

One hand came up to cradle her cheek and bring her eyes back up to him.

"I don't know what to do." Her words slipped out honest and unplanned.

"I know. This wasn't planned on my part either. One of the last clear thoughts I had was on escorting you back to your room and trying to convince you to contact me."

"I remember that, then things got ... different. We stopped to dance. I wanted you to kiss me so bad." She blushed when the words snuck out.

But he just nodded. "I ached for you. When I touched your mouth, it was like nectar and I couldn't get enough. I was burning up."

Rachael found the tears rising again, though this time she was determined not to let them fall. The next thing she knew she was pressed against a firm masculine chest. Her arms came up on their own accord, and for the first time since she opened her eyes, Rachael felt all right. The hand stroking her back was reassuring. She soaked up the comfort for a minute before pulling back, conscious that she was still only wrapped in a sheet.

"I'm sorry." Brand cupped her face in his hand, tilting it up. "I don't like seeing you hurt." He kissed her nose.

"I just don't understand," she whispered.

"Honestly, neither do I, if we were drinking I'd blame it on that we got drunk, but we weren't. Though, I do feel like I have a hangover."

"I've never had a hangover, but I feel so confused and ... odd."

Brand fell silent, lost in thought. When he looked up there was a solemnity about him. "Rachael, I have a friend here I would like us to call and see if he could see us, all right?"

"A friend?" For some reason the question made her nervous.

"His name is Mitchell Adams. He's a doctor."

Rachael felt her chin quiver but couldn't stop it. Brand must have felt it too because his other hand came up, cupping her face, placing a kiss on her forehead before moving closer. "It's all right, darlin'. Something happened to us and we'll figure out what, but it's going to be all right. Please trust me on that."

She found it so easy to relax against him and take in his strength. She nodded.

"Good." He stroked his hands over her back again, and then paused. "I'd like to take a quick shower then we can go to your hotel so you can change." He waited for her to answer. When she nodded, he brushed another kiss against her forehead.

A quick call and after a short hold he got Mitch at his office, who agreed to work them in at the start of his lunch break. When they looked at the time, they had just over an hour.

Brand couldn't believe it was so late. He was usually an early riser. "I need to shower and change. I'll make it fast, five minutes," he promised then managed it in four. Afraid Rachael would disappear. When he opened the door, she was still waiting but dressed in the clothes she'd worn the night before.

The full skirt brushed her ankles. The modest top that only hinted at her bust-line, was so appealing, especially now that he knew what incredible secrets that were to be found underneath. Nothing hid that memory from him or the fact he was the only man to know.

It was a quick trip to Rachael's room, which was in the hotel just next door. Posters for the photography conference dotted the hallway, but the only hint Rachael gave of missing it was a shuddered glance at a poster near the elevator. When Brand looked its way he recognized Rachael's picture and immediately froze.

"You're speaking today?"

She nodded. "This afternoon's final speaker. I'm trying not to think about it."

"Why?"

Rachael hesitated slightly. "I'm not comfortable in front of people. I've been working at it, so I'm not as bad as I used to be, but," she shrugged. "That's one good thing about this." She waved her hand between them. "I haven't had time to think about the talk."

She tried to make light of it, but there was a catch in her voice Brand didn't miss. Reaching over, he caught her hand. "It's going to be all right. We'll work it out." He squeezed her fingers.

She nodded. "The shortest marriage in history." Her voice broke again.

The words made Brand panic. He wasn't sure why, but he didn't even want to think of losing her yet. "Let's not think about that for now." On impulse, he leaned down and brushed his lips against her cheek.

"Ooh, cozy." A familiar sickly-sweet taunt came from behind them. Rachael turned to find Chantell looking her up and down. "Looks like little Miss Perfect had a late night," the woman mocked.

Rachael felt herself flush but refused to back down then she felt a comforting hand on the small of her back.

"Maybe you'd like to be the first to congratulate us. Rachael and I got married last night," Brand announced, as the hand on her back slid around her waist drawing her closer to his side.

The gloating pleasure on Chantell's face vanished. "I don't believe it." Her eyes dropped to their clasped hands and the ring on Rachael's finger. The smug look changed to disbelief then to a look that might best be described as rage.

Rachael didn't have any time to decide, as the elevator dinged open behind them, and Brand hustled her inside. The next thing she knew she was enfolded in Brand's arms.

"Everyone will know that I … I, we." She couldn't say it, but Brand took over.

"We got married."

"We just met last night," she cried.

"Love at first sight," he said, low and husky. "Isn't that what most women call romantic?"

Rachael's lips quivered into a smile as he leaned toward her with a playful smile on his face. "You really are a wonderful man." Her thoughts came out aloud, causing her to blush.

His hand followed the color to her cheek. "You got lucky," he teased.

"I'm beginning to think I did." This time, she said it with conviction, meeting him straight in the eye.

Everything faded away leaving only him and the feelings that had been developing from the first moment she saw him. In slow motion, Brand's hand caressed its way to her chin, tilting it up slightly.

With anticipation, she watched his head lower, never experiencing such desire before in her life. Rachael whimpered as she felt the light brushing contact of his lips before they settled over hers, and she was lost in the magic that was this one man. Her eyelids fluttered down, and she knew only him.

It was the sound of the elevator opening that drew them apart like two teenagers caught sneaking a kiss at a church picnic.

Rachael's blush deepened as two older ladies stepped in, watching them with undisguised interest.

It didn't help when Brand spoke up. "We're on our honeymoon." His arm tightening on her waist.

The two women simply nodded. As the doors closed, one woman looked back catching Rachael's eye. She smiled reassuringly. "Dear, you are in for it. My Jonathan was like that. Oh my, he could make me hot in the darnedest places. How I loved it. Hold on to that man and enjoy it while you can."

"Good advice," Brand agreed taking her lips again in a firm kiss before she had a chance to prepare.

When the elevator stopped at their floor, Brand broke the kiss, and said a jaunty, "Have a nice day, ladies," as he led Rachael out.

Just before the doors closed Rachael heard one woman exclaim. "Oh, that man is hot."

After the tension she was experiencing, the words hit Rachael as so funny, she lost it. First a giggle, then laughter started to roll from her. It wiped away the stress and fears of the morning. She ended up leaning against Brand, wiping tears from her eyes while trying to bring herself back under control.

"Enjoying yourself?" He tried to sound dry, but the sparkle in his eyes spoiled the effect.

She put her hand to her mouth and took a breath, biting the edge of her lip, she looked up. "I think you just made a couple of conquests."

His arm tightened around her. "Only a couple?" he drawled flirtatiously.

Feeling a bit playful herself, Rachael pushed away, heading down the hall. "We'll see," she called back over her shoulder, leaving him watching the saucy little sway of her hips as she walked away.

Brand found it difficult to take a breath. *Man, she was beautiful.* With a shake of his head, he smiled and followed.

Rachael's bravo fled and self-consciousness filled her as she entered her hotel room with him. "You can … you can just." Her voice broke. "The TV."

"I'll be fine, you go change," he assured her picking up the remote for the TV. "Sorry, you only have about a half an hour."

She still felt uneasy gathering up her personal items with him there, but it was even stranger stepping into the shower knowing he was just on the other side of the door. The oddest thing was it didn't scare her. In fact, it was kind of comforting.

Rachael was out of the shower and dressed sixteen minutes later when there was a knock on her door. Brand was just closing it when she opened the bathroom door. Turning back, he greeted her with a tray.

"I thought breakfast might be a good idea before we left."

"I can't believe they got it here so fast," she exclaimed.

"I'm a man of hidden talents."

Rachael pushed back a lock of damp hair. Feeling slightly embarrassed, as he looked her over from the top of her damp head to the tip of her bare feet showing under the edge of her flowing calf length skirt.

"Do you serve too?" The words were thick in her throat.

"Oh, I might be convinced to." His tone dropped to a huskiness which sent shivers through her.

Rachael longed to ask what it would take to convince him but just couldn't manage the teasing words. Luckily, he didn't force it. Setting down the tray, he held out a glass of orange juice.

Chapter Three

Brand glanced over at the woman beside him. He could still feel her small waist from when he had boosted her up into his four-wheel drive truck. It was amazing how fast she got ready. Thirty minutes ago, she was headed for the shower. Fifteen minutes ago, she stood before him barefoot and wet hair when room service had arrived.

She'd looked better than the food to him. Her damp hair had made her eyes look larger and deeper blue. Her skin was flushed from the warm water. Her color deepened under his gaze, making him long to reveal more of it, like he had the night before.

The constant hum of desire spiked, and he shifted in his seat. He needed to get control of himself fast, or he was going to terrify Rachael. Even after last night's experience, she was very innocent, and though his body was still revving to go, she showed signs of needing time. He didn't want to hurt her.

"Do you know how to get there?" Her voice was soft, barely breaking the silence in the truck.

"Yeah, I've been to his office several times. I've known Mitch since school, so whenever I get to Vegas, we get together."

They chatted a few minutes more until he pulled into the medical clinic parking lot.

"I'm nervous. You can tell, can't you?" she asked, as he stopped the truck. "I don't even know why. At least, my heart's not racing like it was earlier."

"I'm right here." He reached for her hand giving it a squeeze, hoping it made a difference. She snuggled into him when he helped her out. He wrapped his arm around her with great pleasure.

The nurse greeted and showed them back to Mitch's office. There, Rachael began to pace until Brand caught her hand.

"It's all right." He pulled her back to him.

"I know." She didn't sound so certain, but she laid her head on his chest.

"Would you like to leave?"

"No." She didn't pause on her answer, for which he was grateful. Then there wasn't any more time. The door opened. The man that walked in was almost as tall as Brand's six-three, with the same lean build, but dark hair, wider features and a slightly prominent nose. He wasn't picture perfect handsome but had a very appealing look.

Brand released Rachael's hand and turned to greet his friend. "Mitch."

"I didn't think I'd see you until tonight."

"Yeah, well I kind of ran into a situation."

"If this is the situation, I wouldn't mind running into one myself." He turned to Rachael.

"Rachael, I'd like you to meet Mitchell Adams. He really isn't that big of a flirt. It's just to give me a hard time. Mitch, I'd like to introduce you to Rachael Jacobs Morgan."

"Morgan? Wait a minute, you didn't tell me about this. You didn't even say you were seeing anyone. When did this happen?"

"Actually … last night. It's a little different story." They all took seats, and Brand cautiously described the evening, conscious of Rachael sitting beside him.

"The thing is neither of us is quite sure how it all happened. I mean, we were getting along wonderfully. I'd already decided to see her again even if I had to go to

Wyoming to do it. But, you know me, and well, Rachael's the same way. This is just so out of character. We weren't drinking. We were just having a last dance, and then everything changed. It was like ..." he paused, "like my inhibitions were gone. I was going on desire and it was overcharged. I'll admit I wanted Rachael, but I'm not some kid that can't control my desires. But last night ..."

This time he let it hang, angered and embarrassed by his body until he felt a small hand on his, and he looked to the beautiful woman who had become his wife. A woman who, with a simple touch, made him feel comforted and at right with the world. Without thought, he raised her hand to his lips.

"Rachael, how were you feeling, any different last night?" Mitch's question drew their attention back.

"Much the same as Brand was saying. The first time I saw ..." She shifted in her chair, "I was attracted, but I didn't think he'd even bother to talk to me."

"Why not?" The question burst from Brand.

She blushed, when she looked at him. "There were all those beautiful women and Chantell was well ...." She held up her free hand in a helpless gesture.

"Chantell wasn't even in your league in appealing to me," he stated with conviction, squeezing her hand. "You can believe that."

She turned her attention back to the doctor. "I'm a bit shy, but I was comfortable with Brand from the first. In fact, when my friends said they were leaving, I was surprised how the time had flown."

"When did you notice the change?"

"We'd danced then came back and finished our drinks and talked." She thought a second. "He offered to walk me to my room. I'm not sure why I accepted. I'm usually very cautious. We were walking out, and they played a song I really liked, and I asked if we could have one more dance. I felt kind of ... giddy, I guess in his arms. Hot–kind of prickly with energy. When he touched me, I was on fire. I wanted him to kiss me. I was actually thinking about what it would be like. I knew it wouldn't happen. Then it was like if he didn't kiss me, I'd die and when he did …" She broke what she was saying, and her blush deepened.

Brand's arm slid around her drawing her close. It seemed so natural to lean into his body. She didn't even notice the slight pause before Mitchell's next question.

"How did you feel this morning?"

Brand was first to answer. "Hung over."

"It was hard to clear my head, to think, my heart pounded, but that might've been because I was shocked and scared waking up …." Again the words dropped and she felt Brand's gentle squeeze. "I was nauseous."

"How nauseous?"

"I was sick then I felt better. It settled down after I ate."

"All right. I want my nurse to draw some blood from both of you. I have two other patients to see while they run the tests. You can wait in here."

The nurse came and drew the blood immediately after Mitch left. Time seemed to stand still while they waited. The room rang with silence at first, as they both sat quietly thumbing through magazines.

Unable to stand it any longer, Rachael stood abruptly, pacing back and forth across the room until she finally stopped in front of the window, looking out, but not really seeing anything. She didn't hear Brand come up behind her and tensed a moment as his arms circled around her then relaxed back against him. A tear broke free when she felt his lips brush her temple. Turning, she wrapped her arms around him, pressing her face into his chest.

They were still in the same position when Mitch came back into the room. Brand started to release Rachael, but the look on his friend's face had him stepping back, turning her in his arms so she was encircled as she faced Mitch also.

"Mitch?"

"You both have what is commonly known as a date rape drug in your systems," he said, straightforward.

At Rachael's gasp, it was automatic for Brand's arm to tighten her to him. Feeling her tremble, he stroked her back in an effort to comfort her.

"How?" Rachael's voice choked out.

"I'm guessing it was slipped into your drinks. It's almost tasteless. You would've never noticed it, and it wouldn't have taken long to take effect. Honestly, the odd thing is finding it in both your bloodstreams. Usually it's slipped into a woman's drink then it makes it very easy to take advantage of her. If I didn't know Brand, I would be highly suspicious."

Brand nodded grimly, taking in what was done to them.

"One thing I have to tell you is that by law, I'm required to report this to the police. I wanted to warn you."

Again Brand could only nod and tightened his arms around Rachael as she choked back a sob that ripped through his heart.

A couple minutes later Mitch put down the phone, drawing their attention. "You're to remain here. They should be here in twenty to thirty minutes."

"Quick response," Brand commented half-heartedly.

"Yeah, well." Mitch forced a smile. "There's one more thing." He shifted so uncomfortably that Brand finally prompted.

"Yes?"

"Rachael has to have an examination. The nurse practitioner can do it."

"Examination?" Rachael felt herself turn cold even before he could answer.

"For signs of force." The doctor and friend tried to keep it matter-of-fact.

Brand's curse came right upon Rachael's response, "No. Brand didn't," she choked out.

"I didn't even consider for a moment that he did, but that will have to be documented. That's one reason I suggested that I don't do it. Being his friend, the police could accuse me of covering for him."

"But isn't my word enough?" Rachael protested.

"Afraid not. A lot of time in an assault or rape, the victim is frightened or too embarrassed to admit it."

"Brand didn't hurt me."

This time Brand was the one that answered. "Rachael, it's better this way." He raised a hand to her pale cheek. When she looked up, there were tears in her eyes. She nodded to his encouragement.

"It's just like a pelvic exam," Mitch spoke up.

"I've never had one before." She looked back, watching the doctor's eyebrows go up, but the lecture she guessed he wanted to give didn't come.

"There's nothing to worry about. It's simple and painless."

Brand squeezed her hand giving her his support. Rachael managed to nod, and Dr. Adams stepped out the door. A minute later he opened it and motioned for Rachael to follow the middle aged woman in a white coat.

Rachael was trembling as Brand forced himself to release her. Her face was too pale. She had seemed tense since they left the hotel, but now she appeared ready to snap. He wanted to go after her and pull her back into his arms and take her away, somewhere where they could be alone.

"Hey, buddy, it's all right," Mitch offered.

"So much has happened to her. She looks so scared."

"Do you think she could have planned this?"

"No way," he stated firmly, but his friend didn't look so certain. "Mitch, she was a virgin. You really can't believe she cooked this up to lose her virginity. Look at her. There were easily fifty men in that club that would have been more than willing to have her. She had no idea I'd press to marry her first. We were both a little out of it by then."

"You really did fall for her, didn't you?" Mitch looked back in utter amazement.

"I ... yeah, I guess I did." Brand met his friend's look straight on. "There's just something right about her."

"Have you told her?"

"There hasn't actually been much time or opportunity. And I'm not sure she's ready to breach the subject yet."

"You ought to let her know."

"I will, first we need to get through this, which may be difficult. I was going to be heading home tomorrow. I can put it off for a couple days, but she's only going to be here three more days."

"That's not much time."

"Don't I know it."

They turned the conversation to the normal catch up of old friends' talk to help the time pass until there was a light knock. The door opened, and Rachael stepped in. Immediately Brand went to her, catching the hand that reached out to him, drawing her in.

"Are you all right?" His voice was husky with compassion as he slid his free arm around her, pulling her closer.

Rachael nodded settling in against his chest again, as if she had been doing it for years. "It's silly to be that nervous about something like that," she whispered into him.

"It's not." He turned his head, whispering in her ear. "You've had enough happen to you in the last twelve hours to make anyone feel off kilter."

They didn't get any more time to talk because the phone on Mitch's desk rang. After a quick word, Mitch hung up. "The police are here."

Rachael and Brand hardly got to take another breath before the two men were shown in.

Mitch was the first to greet them then introduced everyone around. Lieutenant Rawlins was a balding man approaching fifty, slightly pudgy, with a gruff manner. Detective Sullivan was early thirties, styled hair, good looks and more pleasant. In fact, Brand wasn't sure he liked the man's pleasant attitude toward Rachael or the way he looked her over. Though it wasn't anything out of line, but by his actions, Brand knew he found Rachael attractive.

"Mr. and Mrs. Morgan, we understand you were both drugged last night. Could you tell us what happened?"

Brand was surprised they let them remain together when they started, but as soon as he told them about their meeting, Rawlins cut them off. "Wait a minute. Let me get this correct. You just met last night?"

"Yes," Brand answered.

"And married?" Rawlins probed.

"Yes," Brand affirmed.

"I think you'd better back up and start again," Rawlins instructed. They went over their stories several times, having to keep going back over parts until the men were satisfied. Then Sullivan left to get a written evaluation from the nurse practitioner.

It was when he stepped back into the room that he addressed Rachael. "Miss Jacobs, do you feel that Mr. Morgan forced you?"

Brand expected the question, but Rachael exploded from the chair. "No."

"It states here you were a virgin." The detective held up the report.

"Yes." This time the answer was soft, and color flushed her cheeks.

"And you don't blame Mr. Morgan?" The man looked pointedly at Brand.

It was getting harder for Brand to sit still, but Rachael wasn't done yet. "Brand did not force me! We made love. It might have been in unusual circumstances, but there was no force. I couldn't have dreamed for more tenderness for my wedding night or my first time than Brand gave me. The only thing that marred it was the confusion, and the drugs, which I'll point out, Brand was given too."

"And I'll point out, force might not have been used, but the drug took away your ability to say no. That constitutes rape. Would you have had sex if not drugged?"

"No." She looked away. "I wouldn't have."

"Mr. Morgan's drug level was lower than yours."

This time it was Mitch that came to Brand's defense. "Actually, that's easily accounted for. Even if they digested the same amount of the drug, which I suspect was in their drinks, Brand Morgan outweighs Rachael by sixty pounds, nearly half again her body weight."

Rachael turned back toward the officers. "Brand was the one that suggested we come here. He didn't have to. I wasn't thinking clear enough to. I'd never have known. He also was the one who pressed getting married. He wouldn't have had to do that either with the state I was in."

"Are you successful, Miss Jacobs?" Sullivan asked.

She hesitated. "Yes, in what I do, but I'm not wealthy."

"You believe Mr. Morgan is innocent of any wrongdoing?" This time it was Rawlins that asked.

"Yes. I don't believe Brand drugged me, and I won't press charges against him." She met the men's disbelieving looks straight on. "You may think I'm a naïve, small town girl or just plain stupid," she continued without pause. "Maybe I am, but right now, all I have to go by is how I feel within me, and I trust Brand."

Brand could hardly breathe, never had he seen anything more beautiful than Rachael on fire in defense of him. He wanted to take her in his arms and love her for all time. At that moment, he knew for sure he didn't want to ever lose her. He wanted their marriage to last.

He pictured Rachael in his arms every night, across the table each morning. He could see her in his mind walking across the horse pasture toward him, the sun on her hair. He'd reach down and lift her up on the horse with him.

The next image about knocked him from his feet. It was evening, on the porch swing, her stomach swollen with his child. A child he'd never thought much of having but suddenly wanted more than anything. A child, that right now, might be growing in Rachael.

Chapter Four

It was the sound of a text coming that brought his thoughts back to the room, but he didn't take his eyes off the woman who was his wife. Rachael blushed as she met his gaze, making him wonder if she could see the desire he was feeling, or if it was because of what she'd said. Either way it didn't matter. Extending his hand, she accepted it moving to his side.

Lieutenant Rawlins excused himself to make a call. Sullivan turned his attention back to Rachael, glancing at their interlocked fingers. "If you think of anything else, please feel free to call." He held out a card to her and shifted to Brand. "We request you keep in touch for a couple days and don't leave town without notifying us first."

"No problem." Brand fought to keep his tone neutral even though he didn't like feeling he was considered a criminal. Especially the crime they were talking about. Luckily, before he could come back with a smart comment, Rawlins stepped back into the room.

"Finished here?" he asked abruptly.

"Yes." Brand's voice echoed Sullivan's.

"Where can we get in touch with you this afternoon?"

"I have a workshop in," Rachael looked at the time, "three and a half hours." She groaned.

"You might be interested, Miss Jacobs, that call I just received, was another drug rape case. The woman is in the hospital. Evidently the drug wasn't enough, and the woman fought and was raped." He looked at her pointedly.

Brand wanted to curse as he watched the color disappear from her face.

"Good-bye, Miss Jacobs," the Lieutenant concluded.

Rachael didn't say anything, but Brand couldn't remain silent. "It's Mrs. Morgan." He closed the distance between them.

Neither officer made another comment as they left the room.

As soon as the door closed Rachael turned into Brand. He caught her in his arms. Her arms slid around him in a steel grip, holding him as if she was afraid they would be torn apart. Brand lowered his cheek against her hair and rubbed his hands up and down her back before sliding one up into her hair, pressing her head to his neck.

He felt her tremble and whispered into her ear. "Hey now, it's all over." He pressed a kiss to her head. "Shh, they're gone."

"It's not ..." her voice cracked with tears. "That ..." there was another pause where he cooed softly to her. "That woman in the hospital, it might have been me." She labored to get a couple breaths, still clinging to him as if he were her lifeline.

"But it's not."

"No, but I can't help ... if I hadn't met you. It might have been. I'm so glad ..."

Again Brand couldn't miss the fact that Rachael didn't blame him. She didn't even consider him. Her faith was unwavering. He swore an oath he'd never do anything so her faith in him would falter.

Tilting her head up, he used the pad of his thumb to brush away the tears clinging to her eyelashes. Unable to stop himself, he leaned down, brushing his mouth across her trembling, tempting lips.

"So am I, sweetheart. So am I."

Brand was aware of his friend slipping from the room giving them a few private minutes which was greatly needed. Their relationship had been made too public, and he was glad for the time alone. Rachael felt good in his arms – so right. He wanted to just take her away from it all. Unfortunately, there was still one more thing to address. Though he could put it off for just a minute more he decided, pressing his lips to her temple.

A flash of desire shot through him. He pulled her tighter. Running his hands over her, in what he hoped was soothing to her, because it was having the opposite effect on him. Pressing another kiss to her temple, he forced himself to release her while he could still think coherently. Wanting this woman came as naturally as breathing.

"Rachael." He stepped back a little further, running his hands down her arms to take her hands. He felt a shiver of awareness in her that gave him confidence. Her head tilted up to him, her face bright with a light that came from within.

Clearing his throat he began. "I know this may not be the opportune place, with all that's transpired, but I have to say this now. I want us to give our marriage a chance to work. I know we don't really know each other, but I think there's a connection that has nothing to do with the drug. It was there last night when we talked, when I first met you. It isn't just physical. It's a comfort and a bond I felt from the first. I think you felt it too or this morning with all that happened, there couldn't remain this closeness. Do I make sense?"

Her eyes searched his face. Hesitantly, she nodded.

"Good. I understand if you want to back up on the physical … relationship … part for now. I still want you, but …" He paused. "Anyway, if you want to wait until we get to know each other better, I understand. But, I want a chance to court you."

ೞ෨

Rachael was touched by the old-fashioned word he picked. She was also stunned at what he said. It was hard enough to grasp a man like Brand Morgan could have sought her out last night for company, but that he wanted to remain married seemed a little impossible to believe. But then again, maybe the old-fashioned word was the clue. His sense of honor left him bound.

She glanced away, unable to look, afraid what she might see. "Brand, you don't have to say that, I don't hold you responsible. I'm not going to force–"

"Stop! There's no force or misguided sense of honor here, if that's what you're thinking. What it is; is a feeling I want to explore." His hand caught her chin tilting it up to look at him. "I want to see what might be. And when the time comes, I want you to make a decision by what you feel and not on other things."

"What other things?" She looked confused.

He shook his head. "This first." He looked her straight in the eye. "Will you give us a chance?"

Looking in Brand's eyes was a mistake if she wanted to think clearly, but thinking clear and logically didn't hold a candle to what she felt there. She was nodding before she could make the words come out. "I want a chance."

The smile which brightened his face lifted her heart. "Good." He leaned down and kissed her firmly. "It's going to be all right. I promise, and I'll let you set the pace, but it's okay if I kiss you, isn't it?"

Rachael found herself starting to laugh that he would ask her after the fact. "Yes, I like your kisses." She felt a blush rise at her admission.

"That's good to know. Actually, I've never been this touchy of a man. My family is the close, touchy kind, with my mother and sister. But I've never felt this need for contact with another woman like I seem to now," he admitted sincerely.

"I was an only child and shy. I've never really had much contact with people, especially men."

"Does it bother you?"

"No, I like it. It feels good—right." That got her another hug. They were still like that when Mitch tapped on the door then walked in. Rachael pulled back, but her hand found his.

"Everything all right?" Mitch asked.

"Yeah, but can't say I like being a suspect with the police."

Mitch nodded in agreement. "I'd say it's pretty routine under the circumstances."

"Yeah, well, thanks for the support." Brand gave his friend a look of gratitude.

"Hey, we've known each other a long time." Mitch shrugged it off.

"Thanks just the same. I appreciate you being here. It wasn't a pleasant thing to sit through."

"What are friends for? When I need a horse, I'll look to you. Anything else I can help you with?" He looked to Rachael. "Any questions?"

"Are there any side effects to worry about?"

"The main effects are already past. You mentioned the racing heart, that's one of them, but it looked good in your examination. If you feel it again, I'd like to know. This isn't a drug that hangs around in your system, but I would suggest you get plenty of rest. Anything else?"

When Rachael shook her head, Brand spoke up.

"One more thing." He looked down at Rachael. "The other thing I referred to that we needed to talk about. I haven't been with a woman for a long time, so you don't have any diseases to worry about, but I didn't use any protection. I didn't have any."

Mitch got it immediately. When Rachael didn't comment, he asked, "Is there a chance you could get pregnant?"

"I … I don't know." Her voice was almost a whisper.

"When did your last period end?" Mitch cut in.

"A week ago today."

"How long is your menstrual cycle, that's start to start?"

"Twenty four to twenty five days."

He flipped up her chart to check her temperature.

"Mitch?" Brand broke the silence.

"I'm not sure how to say this. I'd have to track her cycle, and even then you can't be sure, but I'd say there's a possibility she could become pregnant." He looked to Rachael. "For choices, we could have you go to the hospital. They have a procedure they do after a rape to help clean the woman out, and I could see if I could get the morning after pill, but in all honesty, I'm not quite comfortable with them."

"Do I have to do anything?" Rachael broke in.

"No, the choice is yours."

Brand tightened his hold on her trembling hand and she looked up. "I don't want to take the pill or the other." She shuddered then took a breath. "If there's a baby, I'd keep it."

He nodded unable to find the words that she might have his baby. Placing a kiss lightly on the end of her nose, he turned back to Mitch. "I guess we're ready to go. I won't be seeing you tonight after all."

"That's okay. I'll see you next month. I'm still planning to come over."

"Great, I'll see you then."

"Rachael, it was nice to meet you. I look forward to seeing you again. If you have any questions feel free to call and remember if you start not feeling well."

"I'll watch her," Brand spoke up.

"Figured you would," Mitchell Adams said, shaking his head. "You're a lucky man."

"I know."

"Congratulations."

"Thanks."

"Now back off. I get to kiss the bride." He kissed her on the cheek. "Give this guy a run for his money. He's a good man," the doctor whispered in her ear.

"Hey, what are you whispering to my wife?" Brand objected.

"Seeing if I can lure her away from you, what else?"

"Not a chance. She's mine," Brand said with a tone of possessiveness, that though he was teasing, made Rachael shiver with pleasure.

At the truck, Brand again lifted her into the seat even though she could have made it there easily herself. This time he kept his hands on her waist and turned her to him as he stood in the open door.

"Are you doing all right? I mean with all this."

Her natural reaction was to say she was fine, but she could see Brand wanted something more. Taking a second to think about it didn't help much. "I feel very confused. I'm not quite sure what to do. What the best decision is."

"Is there anything I can do to help?"

"Can you be patient with me?" Was all she could think to say.

"I can be patient. Will you let me be around so we can get to know each other?"

"I'd like to spend time with you, but I thought you were going to be leaving tomorrow." Her stomach clinched at the thought.

"I can put leaving off. I'll stay until your conference is over." He took a deep breath. "I was wondering if you would consider going to Arizona with me. I'm not asking for your decision right now," he added hurriedly as if to forestall any objection she might come up with. "I know it's a lot to ask, and you might feel better after we have a chance to get to know each other better. I just want you to think about it."

"I'll think about it," Rachael promised.

The smile he gave her was enough to make her feel good about her answer.

"Let's take you back to the hotel so you can get a nap before you have to give your presentation." Brand was tall enough that, as he leaned forward, he still had to duck, so his lips could meet hers for a quick kiss, before closing the door and going around to climb in.

"Is there anything I can do to help with your presentation?" he asked, as they headed back to the hotel.

"I just have a few things to carry down."

"I can do that." He shifted in the seat. "Would you mind if I attend your lecture or is that allowed?"

"You can attend as my guest, but you might not find it very interesting." Rachael tipped her head down, as was natural habit.

"I'd like to hear about what you do." He glanced over and smiled.

Chapter Five

Rachael was surprised she was able to fall asleep, but the next thing she knew someone was knocking at her door.

"I was beginning to get worried," Brand greeted her when she opened the door.

"I overslept," Rachael said, turning back into the room, letting him enter on his own. "I need to change."

"That's fine. I came a little early to see if you wanted anything to eat."

"I don't think I could. Butterflies."

"So what can I do?"

"Nothing at the moment." She got her dress from the closet and hurried to the bathroom. "I'll need to take those bags down when I go," she said, through the door. "I can't believe I slept."

"You needed it."

"I think you're right. Did you get any rest?"

"A little." He smiled, that she might be concerned about him. "Then I went to one of the shops to get a pair of slacks and a shirt. I hope this is okay. I wasn't sure what to wear. I hadn't planned on going out, so I didn't bring anything with me."

"What you had on was fine. This is a photographers' convention. These people are like all artists. They can be quite eccentric. You'll see everything from top of the line elegance to guys that look like they just came out of the woods or off the beach.

She opened the door looking out at him. "You look great." She eyed him over before turning back to the mirror. "The only time that's formal is the big awards ceremony in two nights, and you'll still see everything."

"Are you receiving an award?"

"I'm up for one."

"Really."

"Yes." She moved past him putting on her earrings.

"That's terrific. I didn't know I married a famous woman."

"I'm not famous. My work is doing well though."

"How come I feel there's a strong touch of modesty there." He watched her intently as she glanced away. "Is your work good?" he asked her flat out.

She was quiet a second before she answered. "Yes, it's very good," she said firmly.

"You like what you do?"

"Yes! I like it when it all comes together. The shot, the mount, it's …" She shrugged her shoulders. "I like it."

"What do I have to do to get you to show me your work?"

"Come to the lecture."

"I thought you'd never invite me."

"Well, at least I'll know one person there." She tried to make it sound lighthearted, but it didn't work.

"You really are nervous." Brand moved to stand by her. He cupped her cheek.

"Actually, scared to death is more like it. I'm not good in front of people. The whole thought terrifies me." Panic filled her as she fought to push it down.

"You'll do fine." He brushed a lock of hair back. "But, if you get nervous, just look at me. You can talk to me." He waited for her reaction.

Slowly she nodded. "I'm not even sure why."

"I am," he answered, but left it like that. "You ready to go?" He picked up the two large cases by the door, while she picked up a folder. "You were going to take these down yourself?" he asked once the elevator doors closed behind them.

"I'm used to handling them."

"Used to doing everything yourself."

She shrugged. "Yes."

"I hope you don't mind my helping you. I guess you could say I was raised in an old fashioned family. Even though we all have different interests, we help each other out."

She was quiet for the rest of the elevator's descent. When the doors opened on the ground floor, they stepped out. She reached out, laid her hand on his arm to stop him. "Thank you," she said, swallowing before she continued. "I'd like to have you there for me."

She turned before he could answer, but not before Brand caught sight of the tears in her eyes. He felt tightness in his chest watching her walk away. Following quickly, he vowed he'd never let her walk away alone again. He was at her side to stay. His long stride let him catch her easily since, even though her skirt was full, it hampered her movements.

CB&O

Rachael's heart jumped as Brand fell in step beside her. She glanced over to find him watching her. The grin he gave her was enough to make her steps falter. The man was dangerously close to crumbling the protective shield she had made around her heart. The funny thing was—it really didn't bother her that she seemed helpless against him. Maybe it was the intimacy they shared, or maybe it was a lot more, but she had to admit, she liked the way she felt around Brand. All was well. She just hoped the feelings were right, and she wasn't making a fool of herself.

The lecture room was empty when they entered except for the chairs. A table with glasses and water on it sat at the back of the room, at the front of the room, by the podium, sat her two larger cases.

Rachael felt a rush of nerves hit her.

"Where do you want these?" Brand asked coming up beside her, letting her know she wasn't alone. "Next to the others cases. They're mine too. The hotel has been storing them. They were supposed to have easels here for me." No sooner were the words out of her mouth than two men appeared with a cart of easels.

Brand's hand caught hers and give it a light squeeze. "I'll see to setting up those, and you just lay out your notes or whatever, and take a deep breath."

She nodded. "Eight easels on each side, four across the front and back."

"You got it." Leaning forward, he surprised her by brushing his lips across hers.

Feeling unsteady for a totally different reason, she headed for the water table, filled a glass then took it to the podium. Taking her note cards from the folder, she glanced over them making sure they were all there and, in order, before placing them on the stand. Then, heading to the cases, she unlocked them, lifting out the framed pictures one by one, removing their packing.

"Wow, those are yours?" She hadn't heard Brand come up behind her.

"Do you like them?" She realized she felt more self-conscious than she usually did, wanting him to like her work. She didn't have to wait long.

"Like them. They're incredible. How'd you ever get those shots?"

"Time, patience and a lot of luck."

"Once or twice is a lot of luck. This is talent and the mounting, the photo carries on to the mat making it come right out at you." He looked up. "You don't have anybody else paint them, do you? You're the artist."

She beamed under the praise from him. Her feeling deepened when he leaned over and showed his approval with his mouth. *Brand definitely liked to kiss.* Not that she'd complain, she thought as the jitters cruised through her body. She had been kissed more today than she had been in her entire life. And no kiss had ever made her feel like his did. He was an incredible kisser. He always left her wanting more.

"I like this one." He held up a picture of a wolf with pups. "But look at this one." He lifted one of a mountain lion. "This is wonderful. I want you to tell me about each of them, but it will have to wait. Do you want to direct me where to put them?"

Together, they placed the pictures around the room. Rachael was removing the packing from the last picture when Mary came up to her.

"Rachael." Mary grabbed her arm. "That's the handsome hunk from last night. What's he doing here?"

"His name is Brand, and he's helping me." Rachael glanced his way. Her eyes must have stayed too long because Mary reacted.

"Chantell was saying you spent the night with him, but you didn't." The woman looked to her waiting for her agreement. At Rachael's pause, she lost her calm. "You did. Are you crazy? You don't do things like that. Darling, you're setting yourself up to be hurt. I didn't think, he didn't seem the type to take advantage, and you're always so …"

"Sweetheart, do you have the last picture ready?" Brand came up sliding his arm around her, letting Rachael know he heard the conversation. "Hello, Mary isn't it?"

"Yes. How are you today?"

"Wonderful, this has been the best day of my life. Have you come to congratulate us?"

The older woman looked confused.

"Mary, Brand and I got married last night."

"Married!"

"I thought Chantell would have told everybody by now. She seemed like she couldn't wait to spread the news when we ran into her this morning."

"Married?" Mary repeated. "Are you sure it was legal?"

"Completely, I checked this afternoon," Brand confirmed. When Rachael looked at him, he leaned over and whispered to her. "I wanted to make sure there weren't any more surprises. So I checked, but it's all right." He took the picture from her hands. "I'll take this and put it up." He walked away.

"Married, are you crazy? This just isn't like you to jump into something," the woman protested again.

"I know it seems strange, and it is, but it's also right."

"How can you say that? Can't you see that he's going to take you for a ride? Your work is just coming into demand and will be making some good money. You're an easy target; shy, innocent, beautiful. I'm sure it's real easy to romance you."

"No! I trust Brand. Don't say I'm foolish or anything negative. I've had enough of that." She cut her friend off. "I have a presentation right now. That's all I can think of."

She knew Mary wanted to protest, but fortunately her friend held her tongue. Feeling the need for fresh air, Rachael ducked out the side door of the hotel. The air was hot. Rachael eyed the swimming pool longingly. She hadn't even had a chance to put on her new blue swimsuit.

"Looks tempting, would you like to go for a swim later?"

She hadn't heard Brand come up behind her. That he had come after her lifted her emotions another notch, making it impossible to answer. She nodded.

"What is it, darlin'?" His arms came around her, pulling her back against him. Rachael just relaxed, soaking up his strength. When she didn't answer, he answered for her. "Nervous?"

She nodded.

"Confused?"

She nodded again.

"Something Mary said?"

She nodded one more time.

"I wish I could make it go away. If I could, I'd saddle up a couple horses, and we'd ride up in the mountains. We've great wildlife too and beautiful scenery. You could take all the pictures you wanted, and in the evening, we'd stretch out by a campfire."

"I'd like that."

"Would you come to Arizona with me? We could do that or go on a honeymoon anywhere you want, just name it." Then, as if realizing the pressure he was putting on her, he stopped. "Sorry, you don't have to answer that. We'll talk about it later. We better get in."

"You're right." She straightened. "Can we go swimming before dinner?"

"You bet. And if you do a good job on your presentation, I might even rub suntan lotion on your back." His eyebrows lifted suggestively.

Together they walked back into the hotel. Brand stayed on the side of the room that was beginning to fill up, taking an end seat on the fourth row from the front while she went to the podium.

Panic gripped Rachael as she glanced at the podium. "Mary, did you move my notes?"

"No, I haven't seen them. Why?"

"Because I left them on the podium and now they aren't there." She glanced around frantically, on the verge of hyperventilating.

ෆ෨ඏ

Brand shifted in his seat to get comfortable, stretching his long legs to the side. He studied the picture a couple feet away. The golden leaves of the Quaking Aspen made a perfect surrounding for the trophy-sized bull elk. It was a shot that would make any hunter drool and bring any animal lover to appreciation. Rachael was incredibly talented.

Brand glanced toward the podium. He might have only known Rachael a day, but he had no problem identifying the look of panic on her face. In two seconds he was at her side.

"I can't," she was saying.

"What is it?" He put his hand on her shoulder. She jerked, turned and reached for him.

"My notes are gone. You didn't take them, did you?"

"No, you put them on the podium."

"They're gone. I don't know what to do."

Brand pulled her to his body, feeling helpless as she trembled. "Where could they have been moved to? Did any of the hotel staff come for a last minute check?"

"I didn't see anyone. People were milling around, but they were looking at the pictures," Mary answered then looked at her watch. "We need to get started."

"But I can't, not without my notes," Rachael objected.

"Yes, you can." Brand squeezed lightly on her shoulders.

"What will I say?"

"What you prepared. You'll just tell me all about it."

"But—"

"You can do it. Just talk to me. You'll do great. Relax." He leaned down to brush his lips across her cheek. Feeling her body shiver, his jumped in reaction.

Forcing himself to step back, he gave her an encouraging smile. "Just talk to me." He located a seat in the middle of the room, instead of returning to his previous one.

It took Mary only a minute to make the introduction before turning to Rachael.

CR80

Rachael felt panic as she stepped to the front. It was the largest conference room and was packed. *Why had she thought she could do this?* She caught Mary's encouraging look and didn't feel the least bit encouraged.

Closing her eyes, she pictured her notes and how she wanted to start. The first few words came out shaky. She opened her eyes. With uncanny accuracy, they focused on Brand. The gentle smile he gave her was more reassuring than anything else he could've done.

"I'm supposed to be here to tell you the secrets of getting great wildlife photographs. Well, I can sum it up in three words, timing, patience, and luck, a whole lot of luck. If you happen to be in the right place, at the right time, you get to see the animals. You have to be patient. It's usually not going to happen in the first five minutes you step into the outdoors. I've had times when I spent several days and nights in the woods and didn't get a single decent shot.

"Maybe this is where I should tell you a little about my background. My parents were both outdoor people. They were avid hunters, but they only killed what they could use. That was the rule I grew up with. I don't need to hunt for the meat. I like to shoot but only target practice. So when I shoot at animals, I prefer to use my camera. All the knowledge and skills I learned growing up have helped me so I know where to look and how to track."

She continued. It seemed the time went fast because the next thing she knew she was ending. "In closing, I'll say again, it's being at the right place, at the right time." Her eyes rested firmly on Brand. "Being patient and waiting to get lucky. And I'll say, I think I'm the luckiest person in the world. Things seem to work out better than I could have hoped or dreamed. Thank you. Are there any questions?" Her heart was racing for a whole different reason from when she started.

CR80

Mary, being in the front row, was the first to reach Rachael to congratulate her on an excellent job after she was done answering questions. Brand stood back biding his time so he could get privacy to ask her if what he heard had a dual meaning. Not just wishful thinking on his part. Maybe she did feel what happened was luck and not a nightmare.

He watched people admiring her work. Rachael had a flare of her own. Not only was her photography incredible, but what made them even more grabbing was the mounting. It wasn't until you were up close that you realized it was painted on the mat. She wasn't only talented with a camera, but with the paintbrush.

His attention rested on two men conversing as they moved from one picture to the next, then they looked at Rachael. When the crowd thinned to only two people around her, the men headed her way and so did Brand.

"Miss Jacobs, may we speak with you for a moment?" The older of the two men asked.

Rachael looked from one to the other then nodded. "Excuse me," she excused herself before she turned her attention to them.

"I'm Matt Carter. This is Patrick Holt. We were wondering if you were free now, or if we could arrange an appointment to speak with you."

"Is there a problem?" Brand stepped forward, trying to keep his voice calm even though his protective feelings were rising.

"No problem." The man eyed him.

"Brand Morgan, Rachael's husband." He reached out his hand.

Carter accepted the handshake. "I apologize. We were told Miss Jacobs wasn't married. Maybe it would help if I gave you my card." He handed Rachael the card as Brand read it from upside down.

"Publisher," he said aloud. "I'm sorry gentlemen. Rachael and I have had some trouble here in Vegas."

"Well, maybe we can improve your stay here." Carter looked to Rachael. "We wanted to talk to you about a calendar featuring your photographs and mountings."

☙❧

Rachael felt the breath leave her.

"Would it be possible to go to the lounge and talk about this over a drink, or we can make it for later if it would be more convenient," Mr. Holt suggested.

Brand looked at Rachael letting her make the decision. She glanced at him then back to the men. "Now would be good."

Minutes later, Rachael sat stunned as the men explained they had come to arrange with four of the nation's top photographers for calendars. For wildlife, they wanted her.

"We had originally been contacted by another photographer for the wildlife set, but after seeing your prints, we've altered those plans and we want yours," Patrick Holt explained.

"This was the original contract we were planning on offering." Matt Carter took over, pulling out several papers and laying them in front of Rachael.

Rachael swallowed at the figure listed on the top paper.

"We've actually decided to change that offer raising it another twenty thousand then adding another sixty for the purchase of the prints for our private use to hang in our building. We'd also use them for bookmarks etc., so in addition to the pay out, you would receive a seven percent royalty."

"We'd also use them for a book which, if your popularity goes the way we think it will, we would like to do. In that case, we would be interested in approximately another twenty prints, but that would be a whole separate contract at another time."

Rachael was still finding it hard to breathe.

"We understand this is a big decision," Carter said. "And we want you to have time to think about it. We will leave this copy with you to start looking over. It's a standard contract for our company. We'll have the one for you, with all the changes added sent tomorrow, so you can get it to your lawyer to read."

When Rachael didn't answer, Brand asked, "When would you like her decision?"

"Within a week if possible, two at the most," Carter answered. "We'd like to keep in touch if you have any questions. Also, we have chosen nine of the prints you have here that we'd like to use for sure. There are seven others we're considering, but we'd like to see some of your other work if possible."

"Our production deadline is to start in ten weeks so we'd like to have the decision made within five weeks so that will give us five weeks for layout and text, which will mainly be a brief write up on you for the inside of the cover. We understand you've won several awards and are up for the wildlife award this year again."

"We won't know that for two days," Rachael pointed out.

"Yes, well, after looking at your work, you have our vote. Either way, our offer will still stand. You are very talented."

"Thank you."

"We will leave you to talk this over. We're staying here at the hotel if you have any questions." Patrick Holt extended his hand.

"We look forward to hearing from you." Matt Carter followed suit.

After they left, Rachael dropped back into her seat, looking at the papers. "This is like a dream come true. My prints going national. The publicity alone for my work would be incredible. This whole day must be a dream." Her voice grew whispery. "Any minute I'll wake up and you'll be gone. I'll be alone in my bed like always. No offer and no one to care for me."

"No dream. You're not alone and I do care for you. Just as you said in your talk, the right timing. We've had a lot of luck and now I'll try to be as patient as I can. Because this is the shot of a lifetime and I want to get it right."

"Brand," she mouthed his name. Tears filled her eyes. Her hand came up to caress his cheek, followed by her lips. His arms slid around her pulling her closer as she found the way to his mouth. The kiss deepened until they both became lost in it.

The persistent sounds of a throat being cleared finally register enough to draw them apart. Brand smiled as he saw the color rise in Rachael's cheeks. The smile faded as he turned to the two men who stood beside their table.

Chapter Six

"Detective Sullivan, Lieutenant Rawlins," Brand acknowledged.

"Mr. Morgan, Mrs. Morgan." Brand didn't like the emphasis he put on Rachael's name. "It looks like you two are getting along."

Brand didn't rise to the bait. "I take it you're not here by chance."

"We were looking for you. We stopped by the conference rooms, and someone said they saw you here."

"I thought we answered all your questions earlier." Rachael shifted in the seat.

"We just wanted to ask you a few more."

"How can we help you?" Brand asked.

"Actually, it wasn't you we wanted to talk to. It was Miss Jacobs." Rawlins looked pointedly at him.

Brand really didn't like when he used Rachael's maiden name. Nor did he like leaving her alone with the officers who didn't hesitate to show their opinion of his guilt, but he decided it was better if he left so they could have their say.

"All right, I'll leave."

"No," Rachael said reaching for his arm as he stood. "Brand can hear anything you have to say to me."

"It's all right. I really do have something I have to take care of. I won't be gone long." Brand promised, leaning down to kiss her cheek before turning away.

"Miss Jacobs, we had a chance to look at your pictures. They're very good. Does it ever scare you to get that close to wild animals?" Sullivan asked.

"No, I try not to disturb them with my presence so they don't disturb me. Usually the only trouble comes if I don't give them the respect they deserve. But I'm sure you didn't come to ask me about wildlife photography."

"Quite right," Rawlins said ready to get down to business. "We wondered if, now that you've had time to think, you might have come up with some other details."

"I told you everything earlier."

"Are you certain you have nothing more to add?"

"Yes."

"What about Mr. Morgan's actions? Things seem to progressing quite rapidly, seeing as you only met last night."

Rachael wasn't sure how to answer, but Rawlins didn't give her time to. "After seeing your work, I must wonder again if his motive could be monetary gain."

"I told you, I'm not a wealthy woman." She glanced down at the contract on the table in front of her. Knowing if she accepted it, she would have more money than she ever dreamed, but she quickly discounted it. That didn't hold with the honor that she knew Brand possessed. Besides, there was no way he could've known about the offer beforehand.

"Lieutenant Rawlins, I get the feeling you think I'm foolish, but I trust Brand Morgan. I know he's a man of honor." She could see the skepticism on his face.

The detective showed a little more backing. "We're running a check on Mr. Morgan. So far, the check has come back clean. He hasn't been arrested and has no outstanding tickets. We've a call into the sheriff's department in his area. We're waiting for them to get back to us."

"We also ran a check on you," Rawlins picked up. "You've never even had a ticket. I must say that's impressive. This must be something for a small town girl to handle. Are you certain you're not being played?"

"You're inferring again that Brand is a con man or something, yet you have no proof or even solid evidence against him."

"You want evidence or proof. Maybe you'd like to talk to our other rape victim."

"I wasn't raped," Rachael bit out, but the man didn't stop.

"She was even at the same club you were at. She was dancing with cowboys, having a couple drinks. A guy offered to help her back to her room, but she wasn't gone enough with the drug. She started to fight." He let it hang there.

"How is she?" Rachael choked out. The heaviness in her stomach almost made her sick.

"Physically, a split lip, black eye, bruises, the expected things. She's going to be released after talking to a counselor," the detective answered her. "She'll need some more counseling once she gets home. I don't think this will go down as one of her favorite vacations. Now you can see why we wonder about the similarities. They could've been working together."

"No, Brand came in alone, and he's been with me since. He has been up front and honest with me."

"He could just be romancing you. I'd suggest you be cautious around him even if you won't end your relationship."

Rachael didn't get to answer Rawlins, this time Sullivan cut her off. "Miss Jacobs, may I ask what this is?" He lifted the edge of the contract. "You said you weren't a wealthy woman."

"I'm not."

"I'd say the figure on that paper gives enough temptation."

"I was just offered that contract. I haven't even accepted it yet." Feeling defensive she continued, "Before you say anything else. There was no way Brand could have known about it either. It wasn't decided until today when they saw my work."

"And when did Morgan see your work?"

"About two hours ago."

"He could've seen it beforehand?" Sullivan pried.

"They were boxed up."

"But he could've seen one of your pictures before?" the detective pressed.

"It's possible, but I don't think so."

"Because he said so?"

"I didn't ask, but from his reaction on first seeing them. Listen, I'm not going to second-guess him. He told me he doesn't drink, you checked him, has he ever had a DUI?" When neither man answered, she continued, "You said he was never arrested, but if he was a con man, I can't see that."

"He could be using a fake or stolen ID. We ran it from ID, not prints."

"No prints because you don't have enough evidence in which to demand them, yet, you want me to treat him as if he plotted against me. As I said, I do not believe it. I'll put my faith in Brand Morgan. Maybe our marriage won't work out. I have no way of knowing. It's got a lot stacked against it by the way it started. If you go with the odds of society, there is no certainty. But I'm going to give it a chance if Brand is willing."

"I'm willing." The voice came from the other side of the table.

Rachael looked up Brand. Excitement shot through her as he walked around the table to them. His stride was sure, proud, and strongly confident. Brand was a man whose own worth was above question. Rachael found she didn't question it either.

He didn't ask permission about joining them, sliding in next to Rachael, his arm made its way around her in a smooth motion, letting the officers know he was there to stay.

"Think about what we said," Detective Sullivan stood. "We'll be seeing you."

The lieutenant looked directly at Brand before glancing Rachael's way, with a nod, he followed his partner.

"I can see I'm still at the top of their list."

"Top of my list, too." Rachael didn't try to keep back the warmth she was feeling. She needed to be as honest with Brand as she could.

"That's a list I'd like to stay at the top of."

"I don't believe that'll be a problem, but I don't think you'll stay on their list."

"I'm not worried about them. I'm only wondering, when you said you would give us a chance, did you mean you've decided to come home with me?"

The words she wanted to express her feelings stuck in her throat, leaving her only able to nod, but it was enough for Brand.

"You'll really come?"

"Yes."

His enthusiasm made it easier.

"I want … I need to know if what I'm feeling is real before I throw it away."

Brand wanted ask what she was feeling, but if they were like his own feelings, they were too new to explain and be certain of. So he decided just to be happy she at least did have feelings for him. She trusted him and was giving them a chance.

Meeting her look, he felt a jolt of heat rush through him accompanied with a glimpse from the night before, when he made her his. He wanted nothing more than to take her upstairs and reaffirm their union.

The little voice within him spoke up, yelling for patience. But the little devil of desire added its two cents to say a little signs of affection along the way wouldn't hurt and would be oh-so pleasurable. With that thought, he leaned over tightening his arms, pulling her to him. Rachael must have been at least somewhat on the same line of thought because her chin tilted up, angling to give him total access to her lips.

It was only a second before he was back to thinking about carrying her upstairs. "I think we'd better change and get that swim now." He mumbled after a few delicious moments against her lips.

Pulling back, she looked up and ran her tongue over the lips, full, moist and rosy from his kisses. Desire hung heavy in her eyes before she lowered them, suddenly shy. The lack of pretense in her action heightened his awareness to the point of killing him.

"I hope that pool is full of cold water." The words slipped out.

Her head shot up, color rushing to her cheeks, but a smiled blossomed into a little laugh that Brand felt great joining in.

⊂৪৯

Rachael looked at herself in the mirror again. The cerulean blue one-piece swimsuit hugged her body as nicely as it did when she bought it for this trip. She'd thought it was perfect, now she wondered what Brand would think.

Due to the time of year her tan was lacking, closer to non-existent. Her legs were good, body wasn't bad at all, and she'd always thought she had a good shape. She hoped Brand thought so too. A rush of shyness spread through her, which was silly. Brand had seen every inch of her body, touched every inch. Stopping her wayward thoughts, she grabbed her wrap, sunscreen, key card and headed for the door.

ೞ

Brand pushed himself away from the side of the pool for another lap, but so far the laps and the cold shower he'd taken in his room hadn't done anything to relieve the tension humming through his body. Never in his life had he felt desire this strong. Being Rachael was his wife, he couldn't feel any remorse. He just hoped by her response to him a promising end to his frustration was in the very near future. And he hoped Rachael, the woman, wasn't too good to be true.

Brand stopped, gripping the side of the pool. As if triggered by some kind of inborn radar, he turned to see Rachael walk across the deck. She was beautiful. The one-piece suit was perfect for her the way a scanty bikini wouldn't have been.

Her long hair hung down her back in a braid, but it was her legs that caught his attention. She had great legs, only slightly tan, they were incredible—long, trim, well-muscled, probably from the time she spent outdoors with her photography. Though he didn't have much a memory of seeing them last night or this morning, he knew he would never forget them now.

She looked around the area self-consciously, her bottom lip caught between her teeth then homing in on him, she swung his direction. Placing his hands on the side of the pool, Brand heaved himself out with practiced ease. Not taking his eyes off her, he covered the distance where she stood frozen.

Rachael tried to tell herself to breathe, but it wasn't working. She had married and made love to that. He was incredible. The body right out of her dreams was real and could only be described as a hunk.

Focusing her eyes on his face wasn't any easier then breathing when he had such a great chest. His wet hair appeared darker. Facial features sharper, with an almost predator look, that sent shivers up and down her spine.

"Wow!" he said, coming up to her.

"Yes," she agreed, then flushed knowing she'd said it aloud. Her color deepened when she realized he was talking about her. His eyes said he liked what he saw. He had great eyes. She was staring again.

He was staring again, but it was hard not to and when she looked at him. "Would you like to swim?" He forced the words out trying to change the direction of his thoughts.

"Yes."

He slid his arm around her waist, turning her to the pool, feeling the jolt of awareness that was always there with her. It escalated when he felt her lean into him slightly. Brand liked her reaction and decided, maybe, it could be used to further their relationship. He really wanted her.

ଔଚ

Wanting, hardly described what he was feeling as he ran his hands over her body with only a fine layer of sunscreen between. Her body was toned, curved and incredibly soft. He wondered if she was innocent enough not to know what she did to him. Well, he was completely aware of what he was doing to her.

To anyone watching, the flush on her cheeks would likely be credited to the sun, but under Brand's fingers, he could feel her pulse race to meet his own. Her body quivered with his touch. He learned particularly sensitive areas when she couldn't quite keep back little sounds of pleasure he was beginning to recognize.

A half-hour had passed since he applied the sunscreen to her body, and he could still feel her on his hands. His desire was enough that it would almost be embarrassing.

ଔଚ

Rachael was still trying to get her breath back to normal. Now she knew what the big deal was of having a man rub sunscreen over a woman's back. Brand didn't just rub it on her, like his name, he branded her with his hands.

Touches that should have been innocent because you saw them happening dozens of places around the pool, left her trembling with such longing she didn't dare stand. There was no way her legs would hold her. Did that happen to all the other women? She looked around the pool. No, she decided, seeing them relaxing.

She turned to the side and the man in the lounge chair next to her, feeling another rush sweep through her body. *So this was true, deep lust. I guess it's not a bad thing to have for one's husband. Now, what do I do about it?* Her head yelled caution. Her body yelled to go for it, and her heart was having feelings too new to be sure how to handle.

She closed her eyes ineffectively shutting out the image of the muscled body beside her. Part of her was glad he had turned her down when she had offered to rub sunscreen on his back in return. The other part of her felt bereft at not being able to touch the work-sculptured form which intrigued her so she couldn't get it from her mind.

"Hungry?" The words startled her so she answered "yes" before she realized Brand was talking about food.

Opening her eyes, she caught the smile that hinted he might know what she was hungry for, and then his eyes flicked down her body, and she knew his mind had drifted the same direction. It was a heady sensation.

"We'd better go change." He shoved himself up from the lounge. "Excuse me a second." Before she could utter a word, he strode to the edge of the pool, and his body hit the water in a graceful dive.

ᏣᏅ

The steak he just consumed did little to satisfy his hunger. He just wasn't sure how to get around to doing it. He promised himself to give Rachael time, and never had a promise cost him more. Especially when, with those innocent looks, he could tell she was having similar yearnings. Those blue eyes were crumbling his resolve and

ALYSIA S. KNIGHT

yet, he knew she wasn't ready, but it was nearly impossible to fight her desire besides his own.

The way he was raised called him to take her arm as they walked out of the restaurant, but instinct warned him against it. He shoved his hands deep in his pockets, "I'll see you to your room and say goodnight. It's been a long day."

"You can go." She hesitated beside him.

"I'll see you to your room first."

"I have to go see to my pictures and get them boxed away. I should've done it before dinner, but they wanted me to leave them on display." She was nervous.

"I'll help."

"That's not necessary. I'm used to doing it."

"I'll help," he repeated firmly, taking her arm, leading her toward the conference room.

"Could you get a trolley?" Rachael asked as they turned down the hallway toward the now empty conference rooms.

"Sure, be right back." Brand left her.

The room was dark as she stepped in. With only the light from the open door to move around by. Rachael trailed her hand along the wall but failed to find the switch. In her mind, she tried to remember the location of the switches, but with her nervousness during her talk, she hadn't noticed.

Her eyes became more accustomed to the dark, and she began to scan the room. Out of the corner of her eye, she thought she saw a shadow move. Turning that way, she could only make out the shape of a frame on the easel. Something odd drew her to it, taking her thoughts away from the light switch.

Closer up, Rachael could make out what caught her attention as light from the open doorway reflected off the fractured glass that protected the print.

Tears crept into her eyes as she reached out to it, stopping just barely away from the broken glass. She stood still studying the cracks visible in the near darkness.

A sound behind her came so sudden Rachael didn't get time to turn before the blow hit her in the side of the head. Total darkness covered her before she hit the floor.

Chapter Seven

Brand paused in front of the darkened room with the young man wheeling the trolley.

"Rachael." He was unsure where his unease came from. "Rachael," he called, demanding an answer. He looked up and down the hall. He wondered if maybe she'd gone to see what was keeping him.

"I'll get the light, sir," the young man said, stepping in the room, heading to the corner.

Brand turned back, as the light filled the room, but he didn't see anything past the woman lying on the floor. "Rachael!" Brand covered the distance to her in a couple strides, dropping to the carpet beside her.

"Get an ambulance," he ordered, reaching out to touch her cheek. Her breathing seemed normal, but her eyes remained closed as he called her name. He longed to scoop her up in his arms but knew better. Working on a ranch where accidents could happen at any time, he'd taken advanced first aid training courses.

Placing a finger on her pulse, he looked at his watch, slow but good. He didn't know if she had a seizure or something. He pulled off his sports coat draping it over her in case of shock. "Rachael, sweetheart, can you hear me?" He heard someone enter the room.

"Malcolm with security. What happened?" the man said kneeling beside him.

"I don't know."

"Does she have any medical problems, allergies?"

"I don't know?" He felt extremely helpless.

The man started to ask something else when a small moan stopped him.

"Rachael, sweetheart, can you hear me?" Brand repeated.

She made another small sound and stirred, then gasped in pain.

"Don't move." Brand laid a hand on her shoulder, but it didn't stop her from rolling on to her back. He helped ease her down as she gasped.

"Rachael?"

"My head hurts." Her eyes half opened then closed. One unsteady hand came up to touch the side of her head above her ear. "Someone hit me."

Brand caught the hand laying it down on her chest then carefully ran his finger through her hair until he encountered a large bump.

"Sorry," he whispered when she flinched. Her eyes opened, shifting around as if disoriented. "Brand?"

"Right here," he comforted, stoking her hair back from her face.

"Can you tell us what happened?" the security officer asked, leaning forward.

"My picture." She gasped in distress.

"Easy." Brand tried to calm her, but she continued trying to rise.

"Someone ruined it. They ... they —"

"Shh, Rachael, it's all right," he cooed, brushing her hair again. Her eyes drifted back closed. After a couple deep breaths, she opened them and tried again to push up.

"Stay down," the security officer echoed Brand's instruction.

She made it to a sitting position against their objections. "My pictures, I have to check on them."

For the first time, Brand looked away from her to see what she was talking about. The whole glass on the nearest picture was broken out. The print looked seriously damaged. The glass on the picture next to it was cracked, but otherwise seemed undamaged.

At the sound of the first sob, Brand turned back catching her in his arms. "Oh, sweetheart," he murmured pulling her tighter. He felt her tremble and sag against him.

"Paramedics are here," someone said at the door just before a man and a woman rushed in carrying a couple tackle type boxes.

When Brand tried to release her, Rachael clung to him. "I'm all right."

"I want them to make sure." Brand was almost surprised when she accepted his comment and didn't argue. He moved out of the way, going to the hotel security guard, and spent the next few minutes giving what information he could. He made arrangements for them to find the right kind of glass to have the undamaged picture repaired and the other prints taken care of for the night.

He'd just finished when the paramedic approached him. "Mrs. Morgan checks out fine. We tried to convince her to go to the hospital for x-rays, but she refused."

Brand turned to her but she was ready. "I don't want to go to the hospital." The firmness in her voice was betrayed by a tremor.

"You should be watched in case of concussion," the female paramedic counseled beside her.

"I feel fine," Rachael objected. "No nausea or dizziness."

"We need you to sign a release."

Rachael was reaching for the pen before the paramedic finished the sentence.

"You shouldn't be alone," the woman advised.

"She won't be. I know what to watch for," Brand said firmly, letting Rachael know his being around was not an option, unless she wanted to go to the emergency room.

Again she surprised him by not arguing, but he knew an objection was coming. It wasn't as hard to get her up to her room as he expected. Though, she argued it wasn't necessary him to stay, her strength didn't hold out long enough to win the battle. He ignored her arguments, pushing her into the bathroom with the threat that, if she didn't change herself, he would come in and do it for her.

Five minutes later, she pranced out wearing a satin T-shirt which ended half way down her luscious thighs and climbed into bed.

"You forgot something." Brand walked to the end of the bed, once she settled.

"What?"

"A goodnight kiss."

The "ohh" she made wasn't an objection. He moved up the side of the bed placing a hand on the other side of her. He leaned over, coming down. Not touching any part of her, waiting for her to move or object.

Soft, blue eyes looked into his. Her lips parted slightly. He took the invitation, lowering his lips, brushing gently at first before pressing to take total command of her mouth, while still holding himself away.

The kiss grew deeper than he intended. Either kissing her was becoming more erotic or it was touching only her lips, but he could swear he tasted her to his soul. Raising his head, he waited for her eyes to drift open again.

"Good night." He pressed his lips down swiftly against hers then sprang back before he gave in to the temptation of lowering himself to her.

ஐ

Brand stretch out on the bed. Light came in from the curtains he left parted. It had been a long night watching his wife sleep on the next bed. He glanced at his watch. It was time to wake her again. He sat up moving to the other bed.

"Rachael, sweetheart,"

"Hmmm."

"Sweetheart, I need you to wake up for a minute."

She stirred, this time opening her eyes slightly, almost making Brand laugh at her drowsy expression.

"Do you know who I am?"

"My dream," she murmured softly.

"Dream," he did laugh. "Rachael, what's my name."

"Brand." Her eyes opened, and her hand reached up to touch his cheek. "My Brand." Her fingers caressed a fiery trail to his lips. "My love," she smiled again, drifting back to sleep, leaving him sitting there stunned with desire and hoping it wasn't only delirium that made her think she loved him.

Unable to tear himself away, he stretched out beside her. He lay there for some time before the fatigue of the last two days over took him and he slept.

CRKO

Rachael shifted in the bed becoming conscious of the weight across her waist then the warm body beside her. The now familiar masculine smell kept her from panicking, but it took all her resolve to open her eyes. A feeling of déjà vu hit her, but this time there was no fear, confusion or sickness. She knew the man in bed beside her.

Brand, he wasn't an illusion or a dream. Though as good as he looked he ought to be. Taking her time, she studied him. His sharp features relaxed in sleep were just as handsome. The whiskers that shadowed his chin added to his rugged appeal, but she missed those incredible hazel eyes hidden by lids that were so thick lashed that a lot of women would think it unfair to be on a man.

Letting her eyes drift lower, she followed his neck down to where it flared out to broad shoulders and chest, tanned and muscular, lightly dusted with hair she itched to touch. The hair tapered down his flat stomach before disappearing into a pair of fairly new jeans. Following the line back up, she studied the faint scar on his shoulder. His lush lips made her feel things she never even imagined. She

stopped at the hazel eyes that were almost gold at the moment.

"You continue looking at me like that and my being in this bed won't stay as innocent as it started out to be."

She heard what he was saying but was unable to look away. With a growl, he leaned forward catching her mouth in a kiss that demanded her acceptance, which she willingly gave. Yielding, her lips opened, allowing him full reign. She felt him shift over her. His hot body pressing her down one instant, the next it was gone.

☙❧

Brand stood by the bed fighting to control his body and his heart. Rachael looked up with open innocent desire. He almost crumbled to it. Stepping back, he paced the carpet, strengthening his resolve. He wanted her.

"Brand." Her voice was soft with a low seductiveness which fortunately wasn't always there. She reached to him.

"No Rachael." He backed up a step. "Don't touch me or all my good intentions will go right out the window, and I'll come back to that bed." The words came out a threat, but Rachael seemed to understand.

She rose, moving past him to gather her clothing. "I'll get changed while you go to your hotel and change. Then I'll meet you at the buffet for breakfast." As she moved past him again, she stopped, looking up to him a second before she stretched up placing a kiss lightly on his cheek. "Good morning." She shyly scurried to the bathroom.

"Rachael." Feeling more in control, he stopped her. "I'll pick you up for breakfast here, and we'll go down together."

She nodded.

"And good morning."

She smiled back like a ray of sunshine before closing the door as concern hit him. "Rachael?"

The bathroom door reopened.

"Yes."

"How are you feeling?"

"Fine."

"No dizziness?"

"No." She raised a finger to the bump. "It's tender and I have a slight headache, but I'm all right."

It was his turn to nod. "I'll see you in about forty minutes. Secure the door after me." He stepped into the hall and waited a second to hear the security bolt before heading to his room. He quickly changed to his swimsuit and headed to the pool for a hard swim.

C8&0

Brand was actually finding the conference quite fascinating. Since his family had interests in precious gemstones, he'd been to other conventions. He would have to say photography was more interesting to him. He was enjoying himself, except one lecture on artistry in still life. So he excused himself to reschedule the time to pick up the three mares he'd come to Las Vegas to pick up.

For lunch, he and Rachael grabbed fast food they ate walking along the strip. They stopped and watched the sights. For the first time, Brand saw Rachael with a camera in her hands as she took 'just for fun' pictures together. He kidnapped the camera to take pictures of her then got people along the way to take their picture together.

Playing like tourists, their lunch went long, but Rachael didn't seem to care, wanting nothing more than to spend time with him.

"How many cameras do you have?" Brand asked later as they came out of a lecture about the new equipment available.

"Five. The small digital we were playing with is my newest. It's top of the line and took me a while to save for. I'm really just trying to get used to how it handles. I have three cameras I normally carry with different lens."

"Three." He looked surprised.

She nodded. "Wildlife is unpredictable. You have to be ready when you get a chance. You don't have time to stop and change lens. I shoot as many shots as I can with the one I think will be best then I change to the next for a different feel. I take as many pictures as I can because, with an animal, you can't say hold that pose or turn this way, and you don't always get to pick your lighting."

"Sounds tough."

"Challenging. Sometimes I'll shoot over a thousand pictures on a trip and not get any really good shots. Other times, I'll have several spectacular shots in every set."

Brand could hear the enthusiasm in her voice, but before he could comment on it, they were interrupted.

"Mr. and Mrs. Morgan." Sarcasm still touched the detective's voice, but there wasn't any of the antagonism turned his way.

"Gentlemen," Brand greeted wishing he could tell them to just leave them alone.

"We've been trying to reach you." The detective was all business.

"We've been here." Brand shrugged.

"Yes, well, mind if we go somewhere and talk." He motioned, not giving them a chance to protest.

"This is becoming an annoying habit," Brand whispered in Rachael's ear, following the detective while the lieutenant trailed behind.

Once settled in the relatively quiet lounge, away from as much commotion as possible. The lieutenant began. "We heard you had some more excitement last night."

"If that's what you call Rachael being attacked." Brand stiffened as he felt Rachael do.

The man waved off the comment. "We wanted to ask a couple of questions about it. Mr. Morgan, where were you when your wife was attacked?"

"Wait a minute. You don't think Brand attacked me?" Rachael objected loudly, coming out of her seat.

"Mrs. Morgan." The detective cut her off, but it was Brand who settled her back down to her seat.

"Rachael, it's okay. I went for a trolley. I'm guessing you've already read the report."

The detective nodded.

"Then why did you ask?" Rachael wanted to know, beginning to feel very annoyed at the men's treatment of Brand.

"Just wondering, do you have anything to add?" Rawlins asked her.

"No." Rachael shook her head.

"You saw no one."

"No, the room was dark."

"Do you always go into dark rooms?" he pressed.

"What?" Rachael couldn't follow his direction.

"Do you always go into dark rooms?" he repeated.

"What do you mean? My pictures were in there, and I needed to pack them up for the night. I was trying to find the light switch."

"Did anyone see you?"

"No. I didn't see anyone from the time Brand left me."

"And how long was that?" Sullivan questioned Brand.

"Five to seven minutes. I had to wait for them to send someone with a trolley," he answered.

"Who would have known you would've been in there?" Rawlins jumped back in.

"No one I can think of," Rachael answered.

"Can't you check the security cameras?" Brand asked.

"Actually, they have been checked, but in that area, they're time delayed. It looks like someone either knew about it or was very lucky, because no one showed up on the tape except you and Mrs. Morgan and then you again with the man from staffing with the trolley." The detective's eyes settled on Rachael.

"But how?" Rachael's voice broke and her eyes widened. "You make it sound like ... you think ... I did it myself."

When the two men didn't deny it, Brand erupted. "You've got to be kidding. She was unconscious. You actually believe she hit herself over the head." Brand looked from them to Rachael in time to see her chin quiver. He bit back a curse. "What about the bump on her head?"

"It could've happened earlier," Rawlins suggested.

"Right and she's an expert at changing her pulse and breathing." His voice was full of sarcasm. "I checked it even before the EMS team got there. Why would she do it?"

"Attention, sympathy, bringing out the protective instincts in you." The detective listed back, counting his fingers down like one, two, and three.

"This is a switch. I was under the impression I was the number one villain here. You were warning her all over about me. Something change your mind?" Brand's eyebrow cocked up.

"Several things have come to light. We believe now that you weren't involved other than the victim."

"Well, that's a relief, but would you like to explain what happened?"

After a moment's hesitation, the detective began. "We caught the rapist from the bar. He rolled over hoping for a lesser sentence. Seems he failed his mark because some woman saw him use it and wanted a share so she wouldn't turn him in. Then his target spilled her drink, and he didn't have any more so he still took what he wanted. I'd bet the other woman got what she wanted too."

It wasn't until both the officers' gazes settled on her, that Rachael realized the 'too' was referring to her. She was unable to react, but Brand wasn't.

"What? You expect me to believe Rachael blackmailed some drug off a rapist then drugged herself along with me? That is totally ridiculous."

"Not entirely if you're looking for a good time, but too timid or just didn't want to take the blame."

"She couldn't know I'd ask to marry her," he said pointedly.

"Maybe it didn't matter. It might have been a fringe benefit, a bonus. Maybe she was after money."

"And she just happened to save her virginity to up the take. Right!" Brand couldn't believe it when he realized the officers were actually thinking that.

To the side of him, Rachael's hand flew to her mouth, and she fled her seat before he could stop her. Brand knocked over his chair as he stood to go after her, but a hand on his arm held him back. He glared at Rawlins, but the man didn't release him.

"You better let that go," Brand threatened.

"She's not going anywhere," Rawlins said, as Rachael darted into the ladies' room.

"I still have no desire to hear any more of what you have to say." Brand started to pull away.

"You ought to. We found out who you are, your family and what kind of bank accounts you have, besides other assets. It's pretty impressive."

"And that makes her guilty."

"It makes you a prime target. We also found out you're known as a good guy, the type who helps people out. One who, if he felt guilty about something would do anything to make amends." Rawlins let it hang, but the other man picked up.

"You'd make a perfect stooge or mark for a young, pretty woman who wanted to get rich quick."

"Do you have any proof of this?"

"We haven't made an ID yet."

"Then you have several problems with all this. Number one is—I don't think Rachael knows anything of my family's net worth. We met by accident. I just happened to pick that place to walk into. It was another photographer who approached me and asked me to join their table."

"Maybe she was doing her a favor," Sullivan cut in.

"Believe me. This woman wouldn't be out doing Rachael any favors. This woman's her main competition and is so jealous about her, it's scary. In fact, if you ask me, she should be the number one suspect of Rachael's attack. But, you don't believe there was an attack, do you? You believe Rachael hit herself over the head, set herself up to be raped, or at least lose her virginity to a total stranger, in a night she can't clearly remember. Oh and shall we add, leave her a strong possibility of being pregnant."

Brand's anger flooded out, and seeing the detective take notice of the last word, he almost burst. "Don't say it," he threatened.

"It works though, maybe she wanted a baby."

Brand leaned forward.

Rawlins held up his hand to stop him. "Easy."

"I'll easy you. You guys have such a nice little scenario worked out here you're not even looking for who really did this."

"Oh, we'll keep looking, but you better be prepared for the results."

"I know the results. Rachael is innocent, and I want you two to stay away from her. If you have any more questions, let me know and I'll arrange for you to talk to my lawyer. Otherwise, I don't want to see either of you again." His firmness left no doubt he meant it.

The two men stood, but waited a minute before they moved away. Brand watched them go. They crossed the floor, pausing at the desk set out with the schedules and briefs on the keynote speakers and those up for the major awards. Lieutenant Rawlins picked up a packet and turned back to Brand, tapping it to his forehead in mock salute.

Brand got the message. They now had a photo of Rachael to make an ID with, and then they'd be back. Well, he wished them luck. Because he knew it wasn't going to be the way they planned. Rachael was innocent and what he found with her was real. With those thoughts he headed to the ladies room which Rachael had disappeared into and hadn't come back out.

Chapter Eight

Leaning against the wall, he waited another five minutes, forcing smiles at the women as they entered and left, before the cleaning attendant caught his eye.

"Excuse me." He approached her. "My wife's inside and is ill. I'd like to get her out so I can take her upstairs. Can you check the rest of the room to see if it's empty?"

She eyed him up and down suspiciously, but when he pulled a twenty from his pocket and handed it to her, she nodded and entered. A second later, she came out and asked him to wait a moment and placed a closed sign in the doorway. After two other women exited, she motioned for him to go in. Brand slipped her another twenty as he passed and the woman gave him a smile.

The room was spotless. The cleaning woman obviously did her job well. It wasn't hard to find Rachael in the only closed stall at the end. It took a coin from his pocket to open the door.

Rachael leaned against the wall. Gone was the woman who laughed and smiled with him earlier. Her arms were locked around her middle as if to hold herself together. Her eyes were closed, but tears still seeped through, streaming down her pale face. Brand could see the tremors that racked her body.

She flinched when he touched her. Her eyes flew open and she pulled back. "No." The sob broke from her, but it didn't stop him from pulling her close.

"No." The protest was as feeble as her fighting. "I feel so dirty." The words were agonized. With a cry, she crumbled against him. "I didn't feel dirty before," she said amid tears that soaked his shirt.

He cursed the officers as he pulled her still tighter into his chest, whispering comforting words that belied the aggravation he was feeling.

"I didn't ... I promise ... I didn't." The words ripped at him.

"I know baby, I believe you."

A great shudder passed through her and she clung to him. "Why ... is this happening? I want ... to end."

Brand felt a rush of fear of losing her but refused to acknowledge it. "Don't worry," he soothed. "Day after tomorrow we'll be on our way home." He stroked her hair then tilted her face up to kiss her lightly before he pulled her back to his chest. "I want to take you upstairs. I have to get out of the ladies room." He added a teasing tone to his voice trying to make her smile.

"I don't want to see them."

Brand put a finger against her lips to cut her off. "They're gone." He drew her out of the stall then swung her up into his arms before she could protest. "This is becoming a habit," he teased again before placing a kiss on her startled face. "It's a good thing you're no heavier than a hay bale." He got a forced smile. Rachael dropped her head to his shoulder turning her face in to him to avoid seeing people as he carried her out.

Brand nodded to the attendant and ignored the curious gazes as he headed to the elevators. She had quieted down by the time they made it to her room. When he laid her on the bed, she curled herself into a ball. She didn't even move when he lowered himself to the bed and pulled her to him, wrapping himself around her in a protective shell.

His shirt-sleeve grew wet where her head rested on it. They lay quiet with him stroking her hair and every once in a while pressing his face into it for a kiss he wasn't even sure she registered.

An hour passed and she didn't move though he knew she wasn't asleep. He shifted to place a kiss on her neck. "Ready to go back down?" he asked softly.

Rachael shook her head still uncertain if she could get the words out. She never wanted to leave Brand's arms. He believed her. He made it all better. Made what happened between them right and not something dirty or awful. He made her feel cared for. That she was special to him. It had been a long time since she felt special to someone. She wanted to cling to the feeling forever.

"Will you make love to me?" The words were out before she even thought about them, but she knew she wanted, needed it. She needed to feel alive, clean and desirable.

Brand about groaned aloud at her words, wanting nothing more. He wished he didn't have this noble feeling. But he didn't want to take advantage of her, he couldn't. Not now, when she was uncertain and hurting.

Making love to her needed to be beautiful. Now wasn't the time, though he understood what she was saying. She needed him, but it was his love and support she really needed, not his body.

Turning her in the bed, he leaned over and kissed her deep but pulled back before passion could flare.

"You don't know how much I want to love you." He brushed his fingers back through her hair. "And hopefully soon, very soon we will make love, but now isn't the time. Not when you're feeling what you are. When we make love, I want you thinking only of us and how we belong together. For now though, we're going downstairs to attend your next workshop then I'm going to take you to a fabulous dinner." He dropped a kiss on her nose before sliding off the bed.

Holding out his hand, he waited until she finally reached out to take it. A small smile crested her lips.

"That's my girl."

◌◦

Rachael lay in bed missing the feel of Brand beside her. She turned her thoughts back to the evening, letting the euphoria overtake her. Brand had worked so hard to make up for the police visit.

After the last two workshops, he encouraged her to change into her best evening gown, only evening gown, and had taken her to the nicest, fanciest restaurant she had ever been to. She hated to think what the meal must have cost him, but it was wonderful. The dessert they'd shared was almost too beautiful to eat.

Walking around afterwards, Brand pulled her into a boutique in the hotel and insisted on buying her a new gown for the closing banquet. She had seen the price tag on it, but Brand wanted it and refused all her objections, finally winning by saying, it was for the wedding dress she didn't have.

Rachael held her left hand up, turning it so the faint light in the room caught the diamond. She fingered the ring. It, like the gown, showed exquisite taste. She was scared to know its value, it was so big. She wondered how well he did as a cowboy, but had decided it was too early to pry. Something told her Brand wasn't foolish with his money, but he wasn't selfish either. He was doing everything he could to make her happy.

With one last sigh, she pushed the worry of the police out of her mind and slid into sleep with all her thoughts centered on Brand and love.

◌◦

All day Brand expected to have the police show up. Their allegations were too strong to just let them drop. With the convention coming to a close, they had to make a decisive move soon.

Glancing over at Rachael, he wondered how anyone could believe she was guilty.

He couldn't believe how lovely she was. He thought she looked great in the simple black dress from last night, but tonight she looked incredible. The shimmery blue and white dress fit her perfectly. He knew the minute he saw the gown it was for her. By the amount of appreciation she'd been receiving from the other men in attendance, they thought so too.

Brand felt a fierce burst of pride that she was his alone, not touched by any other man. He shifted in his suit that suddenly seemed a lot more constrictive then it had a minute before.

Rachael looked over at him. He was glad to see the smile had returned to her face. She turned her attention back to the podium, listening to the speaker announce the next category and its winner.

Automatically, he joined in with the applause which filled the large room, but his eyes shifted around. Tension filled him. Beside him, Rachael began to clap and he joined in. Anger in him rose as at the back of the room, he spied the two police officers. Of all the places they had to show up, it was the awards ceremony and just before Rachael's category was to be announced.

"For best wildlife photographer," the speaker announced as if on cue. He read the names of the five nominated men and women. Brand's attention pulled back to the speaker as he felt Rachael's soft thin fingers lock on his. Feeling the tension, he returned a squeeze.

"And the winner is ... Rachael Jacobs."

For the first few second, Rachael couldn't move a muscle as the words soaked in. Then Brand was there, pulling her up into his arms. "Congratulations." He pressed his lips to hers in a firm kiss before gently shoving her toward the front. The applause echoed around her, joining with the nervous beat of her heart.

Her knees threatened to give out, and she wanted to return to Brand. The question she thought earlier about nervous of not winning and winning and having to go up and accept the trophy was answered. This was worse.

At the microphone, she could only get out two words, "Thank you", but the crowd seemed to approve. Quick as possible, she made it back through all the congratulation to her seat. Brand was there waiting, his arm slid around her in a hug and stayed there for the remaining awards.

"Excuse me, sweetheart," he whispered in her ear as soon as the ceremonies had ended and the socializing began. "I'll be right back. Save me a dance."

A brilliant smile glimmered on her face as she nodded before turning back to Mary who was in the midst of those congratulating her.

Brand headed through the crowd for the two policemen. Nothing was going to ruin this night for Rachael. Earlier in the day she had signed the contact for the calendar and the book deal. Now she had the award to back up the publisher decision. Any problems or questions could wait until tomorrow.

"Mr. Morgan," Rawlins greeted as he approached.

"I want you away from here before my wife sees you." It was surprising how easy it was to say wife and think of her that way. "No matter what you think you have, I won't press charges against Rachael, so go away."

Rawlins held up his hand. "Mr. Morgan, it's nice to see you defend her as fervently as she does you, but we're not here for your wife."

"Let me guess, I'm back to the number one suspect."

"No, actually we're looking for another woman," the lieutenant said. "It took a lot of time to get our guy to agree to help us since we wouldn't drop the rape charge. But he finally agreed to look at the photo. Only it wasn't your wife he picked out. Do you recognize this woman?" He held out the pamphlet, pointing to a picture.

It didn't take long for Brand to recognize her. "Yeah, that's the woman who invited me to join the group when I met Rachael. After that, I didn't pay much attention to her."

"Well, it looks like she was out to make sure she was going to get lucky with you or out to get a little revenge for you ditching her," Sullivan added.

"We ran into her the next morning. She was rather smug. And it's more than me. She's Rachael's main competition." His mind raced. "She was angling for the calendar deal that Rachael got. It was her I was thinking about when I mentioned who might have attacked Rachael and vandalized her pictures."

"You think she could have attacked your wife?" Sullivan wondered.

"Honestly, I don't know. I don't know her well at all, but I wouldn't put it past her."

"Okay, let's see if we can find her." The detective started scanning the room.

Brand saw Chantell as soon as he turned, standing at the table next to Rachael. He headed across leaving the officers to follow.

Chantell's attention shifted to him, drawing up Rachael's gaze.

The smile drained from Rachael's face at the sight of the two men behind him. "Lieutenant Rawlins, Detective Sullivan." Her greeting sounded hollow.

But Brand took over the scene. "Chantell, these two officers would like to ask you some questions."

"Chantell?" Rachael looked at him in question then to the woman beside her, and back to the officers.

"Actually, we have a warrant for your arrest." Rawlins moved forward.

"I don't think so," the woman returned coldly.

Rachael started to turn her head to look at Chantell but before she could react Chantell grabbed the steak knife from the table. Rachael felt the sharp prick against her neck. The men froze, as did the other people around the table. Gradually the noise in the room died as attention shifted to them.

"Stand up," Chantell commanded.

Rachael felt the knife bite deeper in to her skin. With her eyes locked on Brand pulling reassurance from him, she stood. Her knees shook and she had to fight back a whimper when she felt the trickle of warm blood on her neck.

"Slowly," the woman ordered. "Don't move!" she yelled as the officers shifted.

"Chantell, let her go," Brand said softly.

"I don't think so."

"You don't want to do this," he continued.

"You're wrong. I should've done this a long time ago. The sweet little golden girl. She appeared and took all the attention that should've been mine. Female in a male dominated category. My father was so proud of me. I won the award three years in a row, but all everyone talked about was the girl that got the prize for the best newcomer. After that, it was always Rachael Jacobs. Even you fell for little Miss Goodie Two Shoes when I promised what I knew you wouldn't get from her. But you got it, didn't you, and you even ruined that by marrying her." The woman's voice had been gaining in volume, now she yelled.

"She got my calendar deal. It was mine. I arranged to meet with them. I should've been the keynote speaker. Everyone knew she was too shy to stand up in public, but she decided to talk." Chantell sank her fingers Rachael's hair and yanked her head back.

"So Rachael got the deal. Rachael got the trophy. Rachael got the man. Rachael got," she yelled, then became very quiet. "But I'm taking it back, the trophy and her. I'll be the best."

Rachael tried not to flinch as the knife dug deeper.

"You need to put the knife down," the detective said calmly. "Look what's happening. You're just getting her more attention. Sympathy which should be yours. If you let her go, we can help you. And I, for one, would like to see your work."

"You're just saying that," the woman whined almost like a little girl.

"No." Sullivan held out the pamphlet. "I saw your picture in here with one of your photos. It was in black and white, did you do it in color? I'd like to see it."

The woman moved slowly. The knife drifting away from Rachael's neck fractionally, but was way too close to take a chance of reaching for it.

"Can we go see it, then maybe get a drink at the lounge?"

"A drink?"

"Yeah, while you tell me about your work. You must have had some great adventures." Sullivan moved up by Brand while he was talking.

For all the aggravation the detective had caused Rachael, Brand was impressive in this situation as he watched the knife drop an inch farther away from Rachael's neck. Brand waited tense, ready to move when Sullivan did.

"What's your favorite spot to go to photograph?" Sullivan continued to distract her.

"I like—" The woman spun, startled by the crash of a tray full of dishes which was knocked from the table where it balanced. Brand dove forward with Sullivan.

Chantell, distracted only for an instant, recovered quickly. She pushed Rachael into the oncoming detective. In horror, Brand saw the knife on its downward arc toward Rachael's unprotected back.

Chairs, Sullivan, and Rachael blocked his way from reaching Chantell. The only thing he could do was dive over Rachael. He felt the knife tear into his left arm and slash across it. He was ready for the next strike to hit him in his back.

When it didn't come, he turned his head. Rawlins and another photographer held the squirming Chantell between them. The knife had been wrenched from her fingers, and it now rested safely in Rawlins's hand.

"Rachael!" Brand rolled to the side bringing her with him. "Darlin'." He snatched the handkerchief from his pocket. Ignoring his arm, he placed the handkerchief over the small cut on her neck. "Let me see." He moved the material way. "It's not bad." He sighed.

"Brand!"

Her cry startled him, but when he swung around in defense, she caught his arm.

"You're bleeding." She surveyed the blood soaked sleeve.

"No, you'll get blood on you," he protested.

"Blood on me?" Her expression said she couldn't believe what he just said.

"It's nothing, and I don't want to ruin your dress. It looks perfect on you."

"I'm not the least bit worried about my dress." She reached for a clean cloth napkin from the table and tried to wrap it around his arm.

Brand took the napkin away from her, holding it in place so she couldn't get a good look.

"Let me see!" She tried to catch his hand, but he pulled back.

"It's nothing, just a scratch."

"Then why won't you let me see?"

"I will, once you go change out of your dress, then you can take care of it," he insisted.

"That's ridiculous." She reached again for his arm, but he pulled back.

"Change first. What will it take you, ten minutes?" He could tell she didn't want to give up the fight. "I'm not going anywhere. I promise."

"All right!" She threw up her hands. "I'll be back in five," she gave in, climbing to her feet.

"Take time to clean your neck," he put in then looking behind her to Mary. "Will you go with her and make sure she's all right."

Pulling the passkey from his pocket, he handed it over. Rachael shot him a dirty look before turning way, with Mary trailing behind. Halfway to the door, she glanced back letting him know exactly how she felt about being sent away.

❧

"I can't believe he just did that," Rachael grouched.

"He just wanted to spare you the scene down there." Mary tried to calm her as they stepped on the elevator.

"I'm very aware why he did it, but it doesn't mean I have to like it. I'm not some helpless female that's going to fall apart. I actually handle accident situations very well. I've passed the Red Cross first aid courses and have even helped on several search and rescue parties back home."

"Does he know that?" Mary asked being too reasonable.

"Probably not. We haven't talked about it," Rachael conceded, striding out of the elevator and down the hall. "It doesn't make a difference."

"You can't fault him for wanting to take care of you." Mary stepped up from behind to put the key card in the door. "After being around that man for a few minutes, you know he's a gentleman and the way he looks at you. Even from the first moment he saw you, it was only you. That's probably one of the things that got Chantell so much. Here she made this big flaunting play, and he didn't notice anything but you and you didn't even try.

85

"Chantell." Rachael paused sliding on her pants. "I can't believe it. I mean, I don't know what to think. I always suspected she didn't really like me, and I always thought she was kind of obsessive, but I can't believe ...." She pulled on her sweater and slipped her feet into a pair of sandals.

"Can you take care of this?" Rachael waved her hand toward the floor where she had just dropped the dress. "I want to get back to Brand."

"Sure."

Rachael was already heading out the door. Mary looked at her watch. Four minutes, she'd make it back down there in five.

Chapter Nine

Brand watched Rachael make it out of the room before doubling over, clutching his arm with the blood soaked napkin.

"Morgan?" Rawlins questioned, while Sullivan finished putting handcuffs on the woman and reading her rights.

"I'm all right." He tried to sound positive.

"You're certain?" Rawlins crouched down beside him, taking out a pocket knife and cutting away the sleeve.

"Thanks a lot." Brand didn't feel particularly upset, but it helped taking it out on the man then dwelling on the pain. "I guess the jacket's pretty well ruined anyway.

"That's what happens when a knife cuts through it."

"Thanks."

"You're welcome. Just a hint, I don't think your new wife was too happy about being sent away."

"I know, but she's had enough shocks to her system. I thought it was better to use a little anger to get her over this one."

"Could be, but I suggest you be ready to apologize when she gets back and the way she left, I'd say that will be soon."

"You're right." He nodded. "I give her six minutes tops. I'll let her take me to the hospital then and play Florence Nightingale."

"We have an ambulance on the way."

"Don't worry about it. I'll call my doctor friend."

"They're already on their way so we'll let them check you out first," Rawlins insisted.

"I'm not going to bleed to death on you. It's not that bad."

"Yeah, but you have to worry about nerve damage and that wasn't exactly a clean knife she used," Rawlins pointed out then looked to the door and down at his watch. "Five minutes. She's good."

"You're married?" Brand asked.

"Yeah, in fact, she reminds me of your wife. Quiet and feisty."

Brand nodded.

"And well worth it," Rawlins added.

"You got that right," Brand agreed wholeheartedly. "You're fast." Brand greeted her as she approached.

"Don't even think of trying to side track me." Rachael knelt beside him.

"I wouldn't think of it. How about helping me up?" He hadn't thought about the fact he was still sitting on the floor.

He was a little woozy as he stood. Making it to the chair, he settled with a sigh. The shock was subsiding, and his arm hurt like crazy. A hiss escaped through his teeth as she lifted the cloth.

"Brand," she exclaimed full of worry.

"It's all right."

"It's deep and you need stitches, bad."

"You could just kiss it better." He forced a grin. "Or you can take me to get stitches then you can kiss it better." He tried for wickedness in his voice and must have succeeded somewhat. Rachael leaned over and brushed her lips to his. It was just what he needed, but she didn't stay there long enough. Then again, forever might not have been long enough. The taste of her was becoming addictive.

"You want to grab my cell-phone out of my pocket and see if you can reach Mitch, and we'll see how his sewing skills are."

"Where?"

"Jacket, right side."

Rachael removed the phone and his truck keys. "I'll take these."

"Yes ma'am." He shot her a cocky grin.

She ignored it as she found the number and pressed connect. Rachael was surprised she was able to reach Mitch. He gave her directions to where to meet him. Several minutes later, after assuring the police that they'd be available the next day for statements, she wrapped her arm around Brand helping him up. She knew he could walk on his own, but he draped his good arm around her shoulder. She didn't comment and neither did he.

He didn't argue when she unlocked the passenger side. He just climbed in and waited while she came around to the other side. "You're pretty good at that," he commented as she deftly slid into the seat.

"I have a four wheel drive at home."

"Makes sense to get off road."

She nodded.

He laid his head back against the door.

"Are you all right?" There was no missing the concern in her voice.

"Yeah, just the adrenaline let down."

Again she nodded, falling quiet. "That knife was meant for me." There was a quiver in her voice, but her hands were steady on the wheel.

"I'd rather have a scratch on my arm then a knife in your back."

"She was going to stab me."

"I think she went a little out of her mind. If it helps, I don't think any of it was premeditated. I think she just grabbed opportunity."

"Why do you say that?" Rachael glanced at him then back to the road.

"Well, at the bar Chantell couldn't know we'd meet or be attracted. She probably was steaming when she saw the guy slip the drug into the drink. It probably really got her again the next morning when we were together."

"And married," she picked up his line of thought.

Brand nodded. "And you weren't crushed. Then the big deal she wanted fell into your lap, so she went after your work."

"And I walked in."

"Yeah and tonight, she realized she was caught, and you'd just won the award. She just went over the edge."

They were quiet a minute before Rachael spoke again. "You know what's crazy? Chantell's won that award three times. No one person has ever done that, and she's only a little older than I am."

Brand shrugged then grimaced. "Some people have to be the top. She was the darling of the field until you came along. Last year she could say it was a fluke you were awarded over her but two years." He let it hang.

೧೩৪০

Brand was groggy when he finally forced his eyes open. He felt a flash of pain when he went to stretch his arms, bringing back the memory of the night before. The room was dark. He rolled over to see the clock, twelve twenty-four. Sitting up abruptly, he groaned. He tried shaking his head to clear it. The pain pills that Mitch had given him, and Rachael insisted he take, had really put him out.

Rachael, he looked around the room. "Rachael." He reached for the light switch. She was gone. He remembered her getting him to the room and into bed. He remembered stealing a kiss, holding her to him, and asking her to stay awhile. She had cuddled down next to him and held him to her. He had drifted to sleep against the sweet softness of her.

Standing, it took a second for his head to clear. "Half the day's gone." Heading for the shower, he remembered his arm and shrugged. The bandage better hold because he needed a shower to wake him up.

Ten minutes later, pulling his jeans on, he noticed a paper on the dresser.

Mitch said you were to rest today. No driving. So I called Mr. Frome and explained that we'd pick up the horses tomorrow.

I went shopping for some clothes, since all I have was what I brought for the conference. Don't grouch. I'll be back before one. If you're hungry, don't wait. I'll catch up with you.

P.S. I took your truck, please say it's okay.

It was signed her name punctuated with a little heart that made him smile. He really couldn't be upset having another free day with Rachael. Especially, one free from troubles, he hoped.

Picking up the phone he called home, not surprised when he got the answering machine. "I got held up another day. Be home tomorrow night. I have a surprise for you." Did he ever, he grinned. "Love you." He put the phone down and was just wondering what to do when he heard someone at the door.

"Hi." Rachael smiled, stepping in.

"Hi." He rose from the bed, walking toward her.

ᏣᏋᎤ

Rachael couldn't seem to catch the breath that fled at the sight of him wearing only a pair of jeans. His hair was wet from the shower. He exuded masculinity. As he stopped in front of her, her eyes locked on his chest, unable to look away.

"Oh, my." Rachael hadn't even realized that she said it aloud until Brand's smile deepened. Forcing her eyes away to find a safer place for her thoughts, she eyed the bandage on his arm.

"I hope you didn't get that wet." She motioned to it.

"I was careful." He lowered his head. "It's too bad you didn't get back sooner. You could have helped wash my back." Brand captured her mouth as it made a little O.

Rachael shivered as she felt the crisp hair of his chest under her fingers. The moan that escaped from her was matched by him.

"I don't mind that you took my truck," he said as he pulled back. "You can have anything you want."

Rachael was tempted to take him up on it knowing what he was hinting. She swallowed. "I'm hungry."

"I'm hungry too, but if you want food, I suggest we get going now." He stepped back grabbing his shirt and pulling it on.

She was disappointed he didn't pull her into bed instead but knew it was still too soon. No matter what her feelings were, she wasn't ready yet.

⋘⋙

Rachael was ready when Brand knocked at her door at eight-thirty the next morning to go to breakfast. It was the quietest she'd ever seen the hotel as they passed through the casino. There were a few people at the slot machines but that was about it.

Brand caught her watching. "You haven't had a chance to play, have you?" He motioned to the large lighted area.

"Oh, I never planned on it. I came for the conference. It just amazes me how people can sit like that hour after hour, just hoping to make it big. I guess I'm not much of a gambler."

"Oh, I don't know. You're taking a gamble with me." He grinned.

"But I know even that will take work."

"Even that's a chance. You're going home with me, and you don't know much about me," he challenged.

"I know quite a bit."

His look stayed challenging.

"First you're kind and caring. You're a gentleman. Your friends think highly of you. The police couldn't find anything when they looked, so you're law abiding. You saved my life without thought of your own safety." She returned his look, waiting for him to argue.

"You forgot handsome and sexy."

"That goes without saying, besides I didn't want to risk inflating your ego."

He laughed, sliding his arm around her shoulder as they continued on. "Do you want to know what I've learned about you?"

"I don't know if my ego can take it."

He ignored her. "You're shy but spirited–very intriguing. Sweet and innocent, but make me desire you like no other woman ever has. You're talented, but not obsessed, thankfully. You're beautiful, but you're very open and loving. Mostly, I just feel very good being with you."

That wonderful luscious mouth was making that cute little O he couldn't resist and didn't even try. The kiss he gave her was too hot to be in public, and he had to fight to keep from going farther.

He tried to fill his hunger at breakfast, but it wasn't the same. They took their time just enjoying getting to know each other better. It didn't take long to pick up the horses and they were on the road. Rachael made a great traveling companion because she could seem to talk about anything but didn't need to fill every minute with chatter. They stopped long enough in a town for a sandwich and give the horses a break.

By mid-afternoon, sitting beside Rachael, smelling her sweet fragrance that was nothing as strong as perfume and knowing if he reached out his hand, he could run his fingers through her hair was killing him.

"Is your arm bothering you?" She surprised him with the question.

"A little." It wasn't a lie because his arm was hurting, but the groan the escaped him was for her.

"I could drive while you rest. I've pulled a horse trailer before."

"You wouldn't mind?"

"Not at all. I'm not tired."

"All right." He signaled to pull over. He got out walking around the trailer, checking the horses, and letting Rachael slide across the seat. Once inside, he leaned back against the door deciding it was definitely an advantage letting her drive because then he could sit and watch her, and she was a lot prettier than the scenery out the window.

"Wake me up if you get tired or want to stop somewhere to eat." Brand didn't really expect to sleep, but the next thing he knew, they were sitting in a restaurant parking lot and several hours had past. Rachael was watching him with a smile that made him burn. "Hi."

"Have a good nap?"

"Yeah, I guess I needed rest more than I thought." He pushed a hand through his hair and stretched.

"Mitch wanted you to get extra rest," she stated firmly.

"And he roped you into playing mother hen."

"Someone has to look after you." She looked up from under her lashes shyly.

If she ever learned to flirt he was in for trouble. Then again, maybe he was in trouble anyway. "Come here," he growled taking her by surprise.

"What?"

"Come here." He motioned to her. Tentatively she slid across the seat. "Closer," Brand said as she paused. When she closed the gap between them enough to get his uninjured arm around her, he used it to guide her in.

"What are you doing?"

"Just getting a little TLC."

"Mmmm. And suppose I don't know what that means?" she said placing her hand against his chest.

He urged them up around his neck. "That's tender." He brushed his lips across her cheek. "Loving." The kiss feathered its way to her mouth.

"Care," she answered before he could, catching his lips fully. The hand in his hair held him there.

"Umm." He moaned against her lips. "Such good care." He tightened his hold, angling her against his body. "How do you feel about making out in a truck?" His husky voice broke the air.

"I don't know. This is my first time."

"Another first, I like that. I'll have to try to think up some more."

"That shouldn't be hard."

"You really are a shy one." He touched her hair, running his fingers down through it, then leaned back to look down at her.

"Was. I'm getting better, but I was what you would call painfully shy."

"It's hard to believe. I look at you and see beauty and poise. I know you're talented. So it's hard for me to see you as anything else."

"Ten years ago, I was a total tomboy. I didn't wear the right clothes or know what to do with my hair. I was self-conscious about my shape." She shifted her eyes down.

"I can't see anything wrong there. It's awful perfect."

She felt his hand caress her waist. "Well, it hasn't changed much since high school, and it was popular to be pixie thin, you know, wear a size one or three. I was kind of tall, not overly shapely."

"Wonderfully," he interjected, pressing his lips to the corner of her mouth.

"Well, I was too chicken to show it, and I wasn't good at flirting."

"It's okay. You can practice flirting on me," he teased.

"I was always more comfortable with sports and in the outdoors."

"And the camera?" He kissed her cheek before pressing her head to his chest. It made him sad to think of her shy and lonely.

"I had a class in high school." She snuggled into him.

"Same with painting?"

"No, that was after. Art in my school was kind of a joke. But there was this older neighbor man. He liked to look at my pictures for something he could paint. One day he kind of encouraged me to paint, since 'I had a good eye'."

"Two of them, both are incredible."

"I love your eyes, too." She raised her head to kiss him.

"So he taught you."

"He started, and when he died, he left me all his painting stuff."

"I'm sorry." Brand cuddled her to him again.

"He left me a greater gift then his paints. My self-esteem. He helped me look at things through the eye of an artist. That helped me notice what was truly beautiful, and beauty is everywhere. It just matters how you look at it."

"You are truly beautiful."

"Thank you."

"You're welcome though I may be prejudice. You know every man wants to think his wife is beautiful, but you sure did catch my eye the moment I first saw you." He kissed her again trying to let her know he meant every word of it.

The kiss was growing a little out of control when a car door slammed next to them, startling them back to reality.

"We have to work on our timing. It seems we always have to go eat when I'm hungry."

What was going on between them left Rachael no doubt what he was hungry for. As hard as her heart was beating, she figured he knew she was feeling the same way.

"Come on, darlin." He opened the door and stood reaching for her hand to help her out.

"I hope this is okay?" She motioned to the restaurant.

"It's fine. Just give me a minute to check the horses." He moved to the trailer.

It was a lot different from the small horse trailer she used. It was what you'd call the deluxe accommodations. She followed him over stepping up behind him through the small access door.

"Brand. What do you do on the ranch?" she asked stroking the smooth neck of one of the mares. Realizing that, although they had talked about the ranch, she didn't know what his title was on it. She kind of figured he was the foreman.

"Well, like I told you, I do about everything. The ranch is mine to oversee. My brother and sister have other interests."

"Then your family owns it?"

He nodded. "For four generations now. It was quite a rugged area when my great-grandfather came there. It actually has quite a history. He was one of the first people in the area. He lost his first wife to bad conditions. He then became so busy building the ranch he didn't remarry again until later in life, a mail-order-bride."

He looked to her and grinned. "But the tale is they were extremely happy together. They only had two children. My great aunt married and moved to California. That side of the family is in the hotel business. My grandfather stayed with the ranch and expanded it. He had a daughter and three sons, but the girl died as a child and two of the sons were killed in the war."

"How awful."

Brand nodded. "My father was the youngest. I have a brother, Dallas, and sister, Candy. I'm the middle, Dallas is oldest and Candy's the baby. Just don't let her hear you say it. She's headstrong and spirited."

"Will I get to meet them at the ranch?"

"Probably, if they're not there when we arrive, they'll be back in a day or two. We all kind of work and congregate out at the house."

"So you all live at home?" She was surprised.

"Yeah, mainly. Dallas keeps a condo in Phoenix. He was married once. She was a real piece of work."

"And Candy?"

"She hasn't slowed down long enough to get caught. It'll be a lucky guy that does. She's a lot like you. Artistic, a definite tomboy growing up, but she's a lady."

Rachael wasn't sure how to react to that comment. She just wondered if that was really how Brand saw her. She wanted to think so.

"Done, let's go feed me before my appetite turns back to what it really wants." He stepped out of the trailer. When Rachael went to follow him, he was waiting. His hands closed around her waist, lifting her to the ground. "You are tempting." He kissed her firmly before releasing her to lock up the trailer.

Chapter Ten

"Rachael sweetheart, we're here."

Rachael came awake feeling a hand caress her cheek and brush back her hair. She took a big breath and was rewarded with the musky male scent of Brand. Cuddling into it, she felt and heard the chuckle under her cheek.

"You're like a kitten waking up, rubbing and stretching. You even make a little purring sound when you're stroked. As if proving his point, he ran his fingers along her cheek again and into her hair, letting the strands glide through his fingers. Rachael sighed at the feel and another chuckle shook her.

Opening her eyes, she found she was lying against Brand. Rachael was glad for the darkness inside the truck as a blush burned her cheeks. She didn't remember scooting over in the seat, sliding her arms around his hips or cuddling into his side. Then again, she didn't remember drifting off to sleep either, but she had done it all according to her position.

"Sorry." She sat up moving away.

"Don't be. You can sleep on me any time."

"I didn't mean to fall asleep."

"It's all right, you needed the rest, too." He kissed her cheek. "You can sit here awhile. I need to unload the horses and get them settled then I'll take you to the house and put you to bed in a real bed so you can get some good rest."

"What time is it?"

"A little after eleven, maybe I should take you to the house first. It'll take me close to an hour to settle the horses. I want to rub them down good and check them over."

"I'll help," she volunteered, wanting to stay with him.

"I was kind of hoping you would." Again he helped her out of the truck. She was no longer sure if he was just being gentlemanly or if he liked his hands on her waist the way they lingered there. Either way it was a heady sensation.

Rachael couldn't believe the stable they led the horses into. It was huge, at least a dozen stalls on each side, and like the trailer, looked top of the line and immaculate. "This is incredible." She looked around.

"Thanks, built it to my specs. I've actually sold the designs to a couple other people."

"Now I'm impressed."

"That's what I was trying for. I want to make sure my famous wife thought maybe she didn't end up so bad off with the husband she got."

"I'm not famous, and I never felt 'bad off'. I feel extremely fortunate to have you for my husband. I ..." She couldn't continue, not quite ready to say how much she loved him.

"I want you to be happy. I hope you'll like it here. Whatever you want, just ask. I also want to tell you that, though we'll be staying at the main house for a while, I've already started building my own house. I've been working on it in my spare time. The framing is all done, but if you want to change anything, it can be done. I'll get more serious about it now. If you think you can be happy here."

"Something tells me I can be happy wherever you are."

"I hope so. I know I'm asking you to give up a lot."

"Brand, what if there isn't any baby?"

"I think we belong together. I'd like to give us a chance, and maybe we can work on making a baby when you're ready."

"Then you won't be upset if I said I kind of ..." she stopped embarrassed.

"Rachael?"

"I'm beginning to hope I am." She stumbled again on the words. "I hope that–"

"You want there to be a baby." He finished for her, unable to watch her struggle to get it out.

"Yes, I know that sounds awful. We're still almost strangers, but–"

Brand silenced her again this time with a kiss. "We're not strangers. From that first night, we had a special bond. Believe me, even if what happened hadn't, I would've looked you up. We would've met again, and we would've gotten together. I believe that," he said it with surety. "Now, we better get these horses settled for the night so we can get to bed."

Rachael felt giddy as she worked with Brand. To think he might actually feel that way. She just hoped it wasn't a dream she was about to wake from, because despite everything, she had never been so happy.

"Ready to head for the house?" he asked, breaking her thoughts.

"More than ready, I'm exhausted."

"Well, let's get you to bed then." Wrapping his arm around her, he walked her to the truck, where he grabbed her bags. Rachael picked up her camera bag.

"You don't have to worry about them. They'll be safe here in the barn tonight."

She looked sheepish. "Habit, I don't go anywhere without them."

"Would you like me to carry it?"

"It's fine. You got the bulky, heavy bag."

"I'll lock up so you don't have to worry about your pictures."

"I probably should have shipped them. I could have gotten someone to pick them up."

"And you'd still have worried about them until you got back and uncrated them," he pointed out.

"You're right."

"I knew I was. Besides it doesn't make sense to ship them to your home if you decide to move here."

Rachael was about to answer as they broke through the trees, then all thoughts of what they were talking about fled from her mind. The building in front of her was nothing like the ranch house she'd pictured in her mind.

It looked like an old southern style plantation mansion—pillars, wrap-around porch and balcony included. She could see the soft glow off a large swimming pool and the outline of a gazebo behind. Lights were interspersed in the landscaping giving Rachael a good view. She couldn't help wonder if the side of the house looked that good then what the front must be like.

"Rachael?" Brand's voice startled her, and she turned to him.

"Brand?" Her knees went weak. She felt slightly nauseous. She wanted to cry. "I thought you said you were a rancher."

"I am." Setting down her bag, he stepped toward her, holding out his hand as if he was afraid he'd have to catch her.

Unconsciously, she stepped back.

"I've been running the ranch for six years now." He eased toward her. "We've some of the best horses in the country."

"But I thought. You know what I thought." She couldn't help feeling betrayed. "Why didn't you tell me? Why didn't ..." She lost words but motioned her arm in a sweeping arc toward the house. "This is why the police dropped you as a suspect after they had warned me you were out to take advantage of me." She felt tears sting her eyes and swallowed them back.

"Rachael stop." He cut her off as the tears broke free.

"Why didn't you tell me?"

"Because, I liked the thought of you wanting me for me. I didn't have to worry about money being a factor as I got to know you. Then I got to know you, and I knew you'd react this way. Intimidated. I wanted the time with you first so we could begin to build a bond."

"I feel like you lied to me."

"Never, I promise. Everything I have told you is true." He stepped closer sliding an arm around her. This time she let him. He caught the strap of her camera bag and lowered it to the ground so he could pulled her to him as he felt the first sob break from her body. "No sweetheart. Don't cry." He pressed kisses in her hair as she pressed her face into his neck.

"I'm so scared."

He heard the words slip from her. "There's nothing to be scared about." He tried to reassure her.

"I don't know if I'll fit in your world. What if everyone think I'm just after you for your money?"

"You weren't worried about that before."

"That was before all this. It's totally different then I thought. I don't think I can."

He cut her off before she could work herself up more. "It's all the same. I'm the same. Just the packaging is a little fancier."

"But I don't fit that."

"On the contrary, I think you fit beautifully."

"I don't know." She pressed in with another sob.

"Shh sweetheart." He rubbed her back soothingly. She sagged against him as her strength gave out. "You're tired." He brushed kisses against her temple. "You need to get to sleep. Things will look better in the morning."

"That's what I'm afraid of." She rubbed her cheek against his chest, in a way he was really beginning to love.

"It'll be all right. I promise. We'll go in. You can get some rest and then you'll see. It'll work out perfect."

Brand gathered the bags and led her across the patio and up the stairs to the second set of French doors. "This is my room. The next room is a guest room you can have." He unlocked the door with the keypad and led her in, stopping to turn on the lamp.

A heavy, carved sleigh bed caught her attention, and then she let her eyes drift over the large room decorated in grays and navy. It had a masculine feel to it, but it was very comfortable. It could have been a showcase for someone who liked the outdoors.

"You like it?" Brand had moved up beside her.

"Yes."

"Good. I was wondering if I could talk you out of that picture of the bobcat. I'd like to put it over there." He motioned to the wall.

"I think maybe that can be arranged, but I'll have to make you a copy. That's one they want for the calendar."

"I can share. After all, I get the artist. But for now, I better get you settled. I want you to like it here. Come on." He led her out into the hall to the next room. Opening the door, he paused then shut it again moving quietly back down the hall.

"Adam, my cousin is in there. It's all right. We'll just go across the hall." He opened the door, stopped and closed it. "Someone's in there, I think its Aunt Elise and Uncle Jonathan."

"It sounds like a family reunion. Did you tell them we–" she let that hang.

"No. I wanted to do it in person when they could meet you."

"So they wouldn't be planning anything like a reception?"

"No, I," he groaned, "I forgot."

"What?"

"The fundraiser. Every year my mother holds a big BBQ. There's an auction. It's a big thing to raise money for the children's hospital fund. I had a sister that died as a baby. It's my mother's way of trying to help that it doesn't happen to someone else."

"What a great thing to do. When is it?"

"Tomorrow." He looked at his watch. "Actually, today. I lost track of the date because I extended my stay in Vegas."

"Today!"

"Yeah, about two o'clock, the auction is at four and the dinner at six." He could see the distress settle over her. "I promise, sweetheart, I really didn't remember."

She nodded.

"You believe me? That I didn't omit it on purpose."

"Yes. You wouldn't do that."

"Good." He ushered her back to his room. "Because this means all the guest rooms will be filled." He gave a half laugh. "I'm lucky mom didn't give my room out. It's happened before, but don't worry. You can take the bed. I'll sleep in the chair."

Rachael looked across the room to the large leather chair. Even with the ottoman, he couldn't sleep there all night comfortably. "You can't sleep in that."

"I've slept there before."

"Yeah, but probably not all night. And not after driving all day. Even if you do sleep, you'll be so stiff in the morning you won't be able to move. I won't have you sleeping in the chair."

"You're sleeping in the bed," he said firmly.

"Only if you sleep there." She stood toe to toe with him.

"Darlin', I can promise I won't get any more sleep with you in bed than I would in the chair."

The smile she gave said she thought he was teasing her. She had no idea, he thought, her innocence was going to be the death of his sanity.

"You stayed with me one night, and I stayed with you the night before last," she pointed out.

He wanted to point out each of those nights were an exception, because the night in her room he was worried about her having a concussion, and the pain pills had put him out the night in his room. But didn't because he really did want to have her sleep by him in his bed. Even if he did have to behave himself, she would still be in his bed, and it was one step closer to having her there permanently.

"Why don't you use the bathroom first?"

"You sure?"

"Yeah, go on." He motioned her to the door.

Fifteen minutes later, Brand stood by the bed, gazing down at his sleeping wife. She was exhausted. And he couldn't help think she got more beautiful each time he looked at her. Sliding in to the bed careful not to wake her, he moved closer and laid an arm over her then froze when she turned curling into him.

"Brand," she sighed, making him groan. So much for the cold shower he just took and thinking it would be easier if he waited until she was asleep. She was trouble for his resolve, but he loved the way she snuggled close.

⚬⚬

The feeling of rightness surrounded her when Rachael shifted from sleep to being awake. Waking up in strange rooms was becoming a norm for her, but there was nothing uneasy waking in this room. Whether it was due because the room was stamped so heavily with Brand's masculine taste or that he was pressed along her back, she couldn't say. What she could say was she wished she could wake up like this for the rest of her life.

She loved him. No matter the short time she knew him. No matter the circumstances of how they came together. She loved him.

Now, all she had to do was figure out how to tell and make him believe it wasn't too soon or that her feelings had nothing to do with the house and wealth. Why hadn't she told him she loved him before? Made him understand that it was the way he made her feel. It was him.

She wondered what he would do if she rolled over and started making love to him. Would he understand what she was trying to say? Ha, as if she knew how to go about making love to a man. Suddenly, she felt so frustrated she could cry. Some woman she was. She wanted to give him pleasure like no other woman ever had, and she didn't have the faintest idea how. On instinct she turned her head, pressing her lips to the arm that curled around her.

"You keep doing that, and you'll get yourself in trouble." The voice rumbled deep and husky in her ear.

"Promise?" She couldn't believe she said it aloud.

With a growl, he rolled her on her back and kissed her until her heart about burst and every thought flew from her head.

The next thing she knew she was shoved to the edge of the bed.

"Go on now, hit the shower." It took a minute to register he'd stop kissing her and what he was saying. Blushing fiercely, she fled from the bed. Some femme fatal she was. So ready to make love to him she was about to burst into flames, and he pushed her out of bed.

Giving into tears of frustration, she laid her cheek against the shower wall and let the water wash them away.

Chapter Eleven

As soon as the bathroom door closed, Brand groaned, throwing his arm over his eyes, laying back in bed. He wanted his wife. Why did she have to learn to flirt when he was at the point of self-combustion?

Promise, promise, oh yeah, he could promise. The only thing was he had promised patience, to give her time. Well, he didn't need time. He knew he loved her and wanted her. And if he continued, even a fraction of what he was feeling now, he was going to be a very active old man if she was with him. No! Not if. She had to be with him. He couldn't live without her. That was why he could be patient for now.

With another groan, he rolled off the bed. Changing into his swim trunks, he headed to the pool to work off some frustration. Brand was on his eleventh lap when a hand caught him around the ankle, pulling him off stroke.

"Brat." He growled when he saw his attacker.

With a laugh, Candy threw herself into his arms, giving him a big hug as she had been doing since she started walking.

"You're home. We were figuring you decided to skip the big party." She stepped back looking at him accusingly.

"You know I wouldn't do that. Mom would shoot me. I just got tied up a couple days and forgot about it," he confessed.

"Oh," She raised her eyebrow. "Your message said you were bringing home a surprise."

"Curious, huh. It's up in my room," he said evasively.

"So you couldn't purchase Miles Majesty?"

"Nope, but I'm going to get a couple of his foals in about ten months. If I'm lucky, I might get a good looking stallion as one of them."

"That's a big chance."

"Not really. I can get my money out of even two of the foals if they end up half decent mares."

"Half decent," she snorted. "As if your horses are ever only half decent. You have the touch."

"One tries."

"So what's your surprise?"

"It's not a what. It's a who."

"Mitch came."

"No, her name is Rachael—" he started.

"You brought a girl home, in your room. Brand, with all the company, how could you? You know how mom will feel. This isn't like you."

"You didn't let me finish. Her name is Rachael Jacobs Morgan," he finished waiting for the reaction and got it after a minute.

"Morgan. You couldn't. You wouldn't. You didn't fall for some casino bimbo."

Brand could see she was getting ready to explode. "Wait a minute," he said sternly. "Rachael is not a bimbo. You're jumping to conclusions and they're all wrong. Let me set things straight. First, you will treat Rachael nice. She's a touch shy and nervous enough as it is, and I don't want to lose her because she doesn't feel like she's welcome here, or that she doesn't fit in. Got it!"

"You're in love with her." Candy looked shocked.

"Yes, she's wonderful. She's gentle and spirited. She's …." he dropped off.

"You are in love with her."

"Yeah." He smiled. "Please give her a chance, Sweet-pop." He used her childhood nickname. "You'll like her. You're a lot alike, except she's not quite as headstrong."

"I'll give her a chance, but she'd better be good. I can't believe you're married."

"Yeah, well I better get upstairs before my bride wonders what happened to me. We'll be down in a few minutes."

"Have you told anyone else, yet?"

"You're the first to know, so don't say anything. I want to tell them. Please, try to help her feel welcome. Rachael really is shy." He left her in the water.

෦෬෭

Rachael stepped out of the bathroom, wrapped up in a big fluffy robe that held Brand's scent. Brand was no longer lying on the bed. In fact, he was no longer in the room. Deciding he must have gone to one of the other bathrooms, she removed the towel from her head and started to work the brush through her hair while wandering around the room.

The French doors were open. She stopped and looked out. It was really beautiful. Actually, incredible was a better word. Right out of the movies. She spied Brand in the pool doing laps. No wonder he looked so natural doing them in Vegas. He must swim almost every day.

She was so intent watching him that she didn't see the woman until she reached him. Rachael gasped as he jerked around then caught the woman when she threw herself into his arms. When he didn't release her, Rachael felt the tears start to well up again.

Pain ripped through her with a load of self-doubt. What was she thinking that Brand could really love her, when he could have someone like the gorgeous brunette in his arms?

"No," she told herself. Brand would've told her if there was someone else. He wouldn't have brought her home. He wouldn't have deceived her. He wasn't the dishonest type. She knew he wouldn't do something so intentional that would hurt her. Rachael shook her head. He wouldn't have said he wanted a chance to make their marriage work if there was someone else.

She froze. But, if he thought there was a baby, and she might take it away from him. That would explain why he had no trouble ending kisses and sleeping by her and not wanting to make love again.

She saw how he talked about his family. He would want his child. But he wouldn't play games, her thoughts jumped back to the thought. And, by the looks of this place, he had the power to take the baby if he wanted. She placed her face in her hands, sinking down into the large leather chair.

Trust him. Her heart screamed, but her heart also loved him. So what choice did she have? She sniffed in a sob.

"Rachael." Brand rushed across the floor, dropping to his knees in front of her. "Sweetheart, are you all right?" He pulled her hands away so he could cup her face in his palm.

"I'm fine," she forced out.

"What is it? Tell me." His thumb brushed back a tear.

She shook her head. "It's nothing."

"Nothing doesn't make you cry. Now what's wrong?"

"I ... I." She felt too embarrassed to say.

"Please, sweetheart, what is it?"

His anxiety was so palpable it caused her to cry harder. "It's stupid."

"What is?"

"I saw you in the pool," she blurted, pulling her head back so it hung down.

"The pool?" He was even more confused.

"With the gorgeous brunette."

"Gorgeous." He paused and burst out in a smile.

"It's not funny." She slammed her fist in his shoulder then sucked on it as it stung.

He caught her hand, rubbing it gently with his fingers. "I'm sorry. I didn't mean to make fun of you. It was relief I was smiling about. I forgot you don't know my family yet. That was Candy, my sister."

"Oh." Was all she got out.

"She's going to love that you think she's gorgeous. And, I love that you were jealous."

When she tried to break his hold and turn away, he pulled her back. "Nah, ah, do you know what it does to my ego to think that you didn't like seeing me with another woman. To know you care. For that you deserve a reward." His kiss caught her totally unprepared.

Her heart went from hurt to overload so fast it left her weak. Not that his kisses didn't tend to do that anyway.

The knock that preceded the door being opened didn't give them any time to prepare for the woman entering the room.

"Brand, I'm glad you're home. I need ..." The voice trailed off as the woman saw them. Her open shock petrified Rachael, realizing how it looked. Brand knelt in front of her nearly naked. One hand on her cheek, his other rested on her bare thigh, unconsciously exposed by the partly parted robe that announced she didn't have anything on underneath it.

Rachael gasped, trying to cover her legs, her cheeks burning with flaming embarrassment. Brand didn't seem at all concerned. Rising to his feet, he walked to the woman bending down to give her a hug and a kiss.

"Mother, we were going to be down in a few minutes, but why don't you come here." He drew her across the floor to Rachael. "You should be the first to meet her. Mother, I'd like you to Rachael Jacobs Morgan."

"Morgan," his mother repeated, her eyes widened in shock for a second before she covered her feelings.

He nodded. "My wife. Rachael, this is my mother, Emily Morgan."

Rachael guessed Brand's mother was in her mid-fifties. Her hair was the same color as her daughter's but it curled under just below her ear. There was a natural elegance about her that made Rachael even more intimidated, still she pulled herself together and stood.

"Mrs. Morgan." She got out, not certain what she should say.

"But, but you didn't say a thing. I wasn't even aware you were dating anyone."

"Actually, Rachael and I haven't been dating. We just met in Las Vegas. She was there for a conference. She's from Wyoming."

"You just met. Oh my. This is a surprise."

"I know. Mom would you mind letting us change, and we'll meet you downstairs."

His mother looked to Rachael. "Of course." She forced a smile past her stunned expression. "I'll see you on the patio for breakfast," she managed before stepping into the hall.

Brand's mother was a true diplomat, Rachael thought then groaned.

"Rachael?"

She knew she must look like she was in shock. She was. "I just met my mother-in-law wearing nothing but your robe and in the most embarrassing position I've ever been in my entire life."

"Wonderful is the way I would describe kissing you. Was it good or bad?"

"I don't think you need me to answer that." She met his tease straight on, a smile creeping slowly back on her face. "I think I better get dressed."

"I liked the idea of you not having anything on under that robe better." His voice dropped another octave.

"Well, I think we caused quite enough stir. We'd better go down and answer some questions soon, especially with all the things going on here today."

"I'm not sure if I like it when you're right." He gave her a mock scowl.

"Poor baby." She patted his cheek before moving past to her bag. "What should I wear?"

"For now, just jeans. If I know my mother, we're about to be put to work, and as a new member of the family, you won't be excluded. Later, it's kind of dressy casual. That skirt that hung around your ankles was great or the–"

"I got it." She cut him off. "Don't give me too many choices just now. I'm nervous enough."

"Don't worry. You're going to be fine. They'll love you."

"I hope so."

"I know so. I'd better grab a quick shower."

ങ൏

"Well, what did you think of her?" Candy probed her mother on, learning she'd just seen Brand's new bride.

"Well, she had just gotten out of the shower and was wrapped in his bulky robe, so it was hard to tell, but she seemed quite pretty."

"Mom, you know that's not what I mean. Is she nice or do you think she's just playing him?"

Emily Morgan thought about the blush. There was no faking it. "Yes, she seems nice enough, and I think maybe she'll be good for him."

"Brand said she was shy," Candy said.

"She can't be too shy if she landed him in less than five days," Dallas pointed out sarcastically.

"We don't know what happened so we'll just have to give her the benefit of the doubt for Brand's sake. We don't want to end up hurting him," Emily said firmly. "Now let's change subjects before they come down here and hear us."

"Brand's going to know we're talking about them," Candy said with certainty.

"Yes, but we don't have to make Rachael uncomfortable."

ങ൏

Brand felt her hesitate again. "Is something wrong?"

"Nothing that being a hundred miles away wouldn't cure, no make that four hundred, anyone for four hundred."

"You're still nervous."

"I'm way past nervous. I've hit downright terrified." The panicked look in her eyes said she wasn't kidding. "I can't do this." She took a step back, and Brand could tell she was ready to run.

"My poor baby," he said gently, putting his arm around her shoulder, easing her to him. "You can do this. It will be all right, I promise."

"You keep saying that." Tension was evident in her voice.

"I haven't broken a promise yet, have I? So you better start believing me."

"I'm trying to, but it's so hard when I'm about to meet my new in-laws and have to face a hundred people at a party, and I don't know a single one."

"Actually, it'll probably be closer to two or three hundred and you know me."

"You're not helping."

"I'll stay close the whole time, and if you need me, I'll be there," he promised, placing a kiss on her forehead and rubbing his hand up and down her arms.

"I'm holding you to that."

"You can hold me anywhere." Again he tried to pull a smile out of her. When it was slow in coming, he switched to a backup plan, a sneak attack, kissing her soundly, "For luck."

She was still a little dazed as he led her to the patio. To one side seven people were clustered around a large glass top table, shaded by a flower laden, lattice awning.

"I hope we didn't hold everyone up too long," Brand greeted, but the attention was focused on Rachael. "Everyone, I'd like you to meet Rachael."

Brand went around the table introducing the people there. His two male cousins were about his age and greeted her warmly, as did his aunt and uncle. Candy came around to give her a hug. Brand's mother also greeted her warmly, inviting her to sit next to her.

Rachael began to lose some of the discomfort she'd felt from their earlier meeting. Only Brand's brother, Dallas, remained cool. His look dissected her as if looking for flaws. Rachael wondered if something was wrong with her make-up. Following her norm, she didn't wear much. Maybe it showed how unaccustomed she was at wearing it, or had her hair went weird? Maybe she should have left it down instead of pulling it up.

She was about to hyperventilate when she felt Brand's hand slide over hers giving it a squeeze. Rachael turned to him automatically to receive a smile. Missing the question asked of her.

"Pardon?" She turned back toward Dallas.

"I was wondering what you do for a living?"

"I'm a photographer."

"Do you have your own studio or do you do it at a chain store?" Dallas questioned.

"Wrong kind of photography, brother." Brand jumped in, annoyed at Dallas's tone. He guessed he should have expected it. Dallas was a bit over-protective, tending to take their father's place, even though he and Candy were grown. Dallas also had his bad experience that tainted things with women.

He would have to talk to him later when they were alone. "Rachael is a wildlife photographer. That's why she was in Las Vegas, for a photography conference. She was one of the keynote speakers and went away with the award for the top wildlife photographer. It was quite an evening." He enjoyed Rachael's blush.

"You were there?" Candy asked.

"Yeah, it was just two nights ago. I wouldn't miss it for the world, especially with the kind of cutthroat competition that it was." Making his own private joke, but when he saw the glimmer in Rachael's eye, he knew he was about to get it back.

"Brand was a real lifesaver. He took the knife meant for me and has sixteen of Mitch's neat little stitches to prove it."

He knew she saw it as a way to get the attention off her, and it succeeded wonderfully.

"You got stitches?" Candy asked at the same time Dallas demanded, "What happened?"

Followed by his mother. "Are you all right?"

"I'm fine," he answered his mother first. "It was just a little cut on my arm. No tendon damage or anything serious. Mitch said I could get the stitches out in a week to ten days."

"What happened?" Dallas repeated.

"To make the story short, one of the other photographers in Rachael's field kind of cracked when Rachael was receiving all the attention. First with me, then Rachael got a calendar and book deal the other woman was vying for. She vandalized several of Rachael's pictures then attacked her."

"Oh my," his mother gasped.

"Yeah, at the awards banquet when Rachael was announced the winner, she came after Rachael with a knife." He shrugged as if to end it only to have to spend the next fifteen minutes going over it in more detail. Brand mentioned that Chantell drugged them but not what happened and luckily no one pressed when he assured them. "Mitch said there would be no after effects from the drug."

"You two had an exciting start on life together," his uncle commented.

"Not by my choice. I tend to like things calm and simple," Rachael spoke up.

"Well, I'm afraid you won't get that today. In fact, we better get this show on the road. The caterer will be here in," Emily Morgan looked at her watch, "three hours. Boys, you're in charge of getting the tables and chairs out of storage. The platforms are already in place. Candy, Martha has the linens already if you'll help her."

"Mrs. Morgan," the maid stepped out on the patio. "The flowers have arrived."

"Perfect, Rachael will you help?"

Chapter Twelve

Rachael found herself ushered off in the opposite direction of Brand, but soon, she lost herself in the hustle. Receiving a full share of Emily Morgan's special warmth, she was asked about her family and life. They talked about the outdoors. Emily talked of some of the places around she thought Rachael might like to photograph and that Brand probably thought the same thing.

As they were setting up the items on display to be auctioned off later, Rachael couldn't believe some of the items donated. It was like no bake sale, auction, fundraiser she had ever attended. There were a number of pricey antique pieces, artwork from artists she recognized and a lot whom she didn't. There were a couple of celebrity donated items that she could hardly believe.

"I would like to see your work." Emily commented while they worked.

"When you get some free time, I'd love to show you, maybe tomorrow?" Rachael laughed. "That is, if we're not too worn out."

"You mean you have some here?"

Rachael nodded. "Twenty-two pieces I used for my presentation and display. Brand put them in the truck and was going to pull it into the garage until we had time to do something with them."

"Well, how about taking a break then, so we can go see them now?" Brand's mother suggested.

"Sure."

"Beth, Candy, would you like to take a break with us? Rachael is going to show me some of her pictures," Emily called to Brand's aunt and sister.

"I'd love to see." Beth came over with Candy.

"Count me in," Candy said and the four headed for the garage.

"I didn't expect crates," Candy commented at the wooden boxes.

"Is it going to be a lot of trouble getting them out?" Emily asked.

"Not at all. A friend of mine helped me build them for easy access, if you have the combination." Rachael opened the lock, then top. "The cases are waterproof with padded sides so not to mar the frames. The bigger cases each hold five pictures. The small holds six." Rachael lifted one out and pulled back the cover.

"Oh my." Was Brand's mother's reaction.

"Wow," Candy's comment.

"That's incredible," came from Beth.

"When Brand said you took pictures, I didn't expect anything like this," Candy said in awe. "How did you ever get a picture like that?"

"Luck and a lot of patience," Rachael answered.

"And talent." The male voice added as Brand walked closer. "What does a guy have to do to get invited to this private showing?"

"You've already seen them," Rachael returned.

"Yeah, but as I'm your number one fan, that has to count for something."

"You would think so wouldn't you? I thought you were working."

"Everyone decided we were all set and deserted me."

"Well." She paused a second as if to think. "In that case, I guess you can join us. If you help, that is."

"Your wish is my command," he continued toward her until he stood over her, snaking out a hand, he caught her around the waist. At the same time, his head came down. At the touch of his lips, she sagged against him.

"Did I wish for that?" she asked softly, when he lifted his head.

"If you didn't, then I sure did," he muttered before reclaiming her lips.

"Newlyweds," Candy's comment had Rachael springing back from him, her face flaming with color, while Brand turned to his sister. "Thanks a lot, brat. I was enjoying that."

"We could tell, but we'd like to see some more of Rachael's artwork, not yours."

The group spent the next twenty minutes sitting around talking about her photos and some of the stories behind them. In that time Rachael really began to relax, surrounded in what she was familiar with and loved.

"Well, I certainly got a talented new daughter, but that doesn't surprise me," Emily said getting ready to go in. "You certainly know how to pick them." She patted Brand's arm.

"Yeah, and it was at first glance," he answered, his eyes burning for Rachael.

Candy gave him a funny look, shrugged her shoulders and joined their mom and aunt in the house.

"How are you surviving?" he asked Rachael when they were alone.

"Much better than I thought. Your family is wonderful. They've made me feel so welcome. I've had a great time."

"I knew you didn't have anything to worry about. My mother can spot a phony person at a hundred yards. She wasn't at all happy when she met Dallas's wife though she tried not to show it, but she really likes you. I can tell." He slid his arms around her back.

"I hope so."

"No worries."

"What's to worry about, just an afternoon full of people I don't know."

Brand smiled and kissed her nose. "It'll be fine. Have you noticed anything you want for our house?"

Rachael liked the way he said 'our'. "I haven't really looked."

"Well, do. My mother always expects me to buy something to help keep the bidding going, though it's written off the ranch account." He tightened his hold. "I really am beginning to like this." His voice dropped low and sexy as he pressed a kiss to her temple. "Am I coming on too strong?" He continued little kisses down her cheek.

"No," Rachael whispered, when she found her voice. "It's just. I can't … think when you do that. I feel … like, I'm going to melt."

"Melt, ah."

She nodded as he continued the little brushes with his lips.

"I'm hot. I feel shaky."

"Sounds like the flu," he murmured back.

"The flu doesn't feel this good." She turned her head to meet his lips.

"Brand," Dallas called his name from outside the garage.

This time it was Brand that broke the kiss. Rachael could do no more than lean against him and try to breathe.

His hands stroked her back. "We have to do something about my family's timing." Even as he said it, he was thankful. He didn't want to make love to Rachael in the garage, no matter how nice it was, at least not yet.

Dallas stepped around the open door. "Can you help me down at the platform? We just had another auction piece arrive."

"Be right there." He waited for Dallas to turn away. "Can I persuade you back into what we were talking about?"

"Actually, I wanted to talk about something before we got ... distracted."

"Distracted?" Brand loved how it was hard for her to get the word out.

Rachael ignored his tease. "I was wondering, do you think your mother would accept one of my pictures for the auction? I know compared to some of the other items, it's not ..."

He silenced her with a kiss, which was becoming a habit, when he didn't want to hear what she was going to say. "Have I told you how wonderful you are? My mother will be thrilled to have one. Which do you have in mind?"

"I was thinking of the mountain sheep or the wood ducks."

"Either would be terrific," he agreed.

"There's one thing, I need to see if I can get hold of Mr. Carter or Holt. They were interested in both of those but wanted to see some of the others in the same set first. Would it be okay if I called them?"

He gave her a frown. "Rachael, this is your home now. You don't have to ask. Understand?"

She nodded.

"All right, off you go." He headed out to find Dallas.

Rachael had no trouble reaching Mr. Carter on the cell phone number he gave her. He was not only willing to give one of the pictures but was excited about the publicity prospect. And after leaving her on hold for only two minutes, came back to say that the company would pledge ten thousand dollars to the charity if whoever purchased the picture would allow it still to be used in the book with a write up.

Rachael went to find Mrs. Morgan to tell her about the pledge and get a number where the paperwork could be sent.

"You know, Rachael, you can call me, Emily or even mom if you'd like," she returned when Rachael called her uildeading.

Mrs. Morgan. "I have a feeling we're going to be good friends."

"I hope so. You have made me feel very comfortable."

"And you were worried," she said with understanding.

Rachael nodded. "It's all so sudden, and I didn't know about all this." She lifted her hands to motion all around her. "I wasn't sure what you'd think of me."

"Well, you can quit worrying. I like you. And I think you and Brand go great together. I do think something else is bothering you, though." She held up her hand. "You don't have to tell what it is, but I think you two would have ended up together anyway."

"Brand didn't tell you," Rachael asked hesitantly.

"No, and you don't have to either." The older woman paused as if sensing something, "unless you need to talk to someone."

Rachael felt the tears rising. "Actually, I do, I know there not time now, maybe later."

Emily cut her off. "There's time now." She took her hand, leading her into the library closing and locking the door behind them.

As the tears broke free, Rachael found herself in a warm motherly hug. "I'm sorry," Rachael said, after a few minutes, feeling embarrassed.

"Do you want to talk about it?"

She nodded. "I know Brand won't mind. Brand and I met at the club like we said, but what he left out is just before the evening ended that was when someone slipped a drug into our drinks."

Emily took a deep breath.

"Brand had already said he wanted to get in touch with me. He had even given me his address so I could be the one to make contact so not to scare me, but anyway. We were dancing and the drug made things a little hot when he kissed me. When I said I never, that I was waiting for marriage, he said we better get married quick then. The next morning we woke up together, married."

"Heavens." The comment escaped her.

"It was all quite a blur, the drug made me sick." Rachael rambled. "Then we went to see Mitch. He's who found the drug. It was a date-rape drug so he had to report it to the police. There was an investigation. First, they thought it was Brand, then me, and then they found out it was the woman who attacked me."

"You really have gone through a lot."

"I'm okay with it really. Brand has been wonderful but." She broke off unable to continue. Afraid the tears that choked her throat would surface.

"But?"

"I don't know how he really feels. He's been great, saying he wants to be with me, that he wants a chance for our marriage to work. I'm worried, it's just that … there's a pretty strong chance I may be pregnant."

Emily caught her breath. "How are you feeling?"

"Fine, I think. It's been quite strange lately."

"That's a lot to go through. I don't blame you for being unsettled with what's been happening."

"Actually, as I said, I've come to terms with it mostly. It's just." Taking a breath, Rachael continued. "Brand and I haven't … slept together. I mean we slept last night, but we haven't …" she couldn't go on. She tried to pull away, wishing she had never tried to confide in his mother.

"You haven't made love." Emily finished for her.

Rachael shook with tears.

"And you want to."

Rachael managed a nod as Emily continued.

"You've fallen in love with Brand."

"Yes." The teary answer was ripped from her as she found herself in another hug.

"Have you told him?" Emily leaned back brushing away a tear.

"I've tried. He wants me to take my time to be sure."

"But you're sure already."

"Yes, but … I don't even know how to seduce my own husband into making love to me," Rachael cried out, bring a smile to the older woman's face.

"I don't think that will be much of a problem. I've seen the way my son looks at you, the way he kissed you. Trust me, I've known him a long time, you could say. He has never looked at a woman the way he looks at you. My son's in love with you, and I couldn't be more pleased. I think you two will do great together."

"You do?"

"Yes."

"Then what should I do?"

"Let nature take its course and tell him how you feel. I don't think it will be hard when the time comes."

Rachael threw her arms around her new mother-in-law. "Thank you." The tears this time were happy ones. "Sorry," she pulled back.

"Don't be." Emily waved it off, wiping at her eyes. "Feel free to give me a hug anytime you want." She gave her a hug to back up her words. "Now we better do the last minute things before guest arrive."

"Oh, that's why I was looking for you. Would you like one of my pictures to add to the auction? Even if it doesn't bring much, the publishing company promised ten thousand dollars if whoever purchases it will allow it to be used in the book."

"Oh my, that's wonderful. I knew you were special." She gave Rachael another hug. "Thank you."

"You're welcome."

"Which picture?"

"I've decided on the mountain sheep. It should appeal to the men for their offices. You know strong, rugged." Rachael smiled.

"Good choice."

"I just need a fax number if you have one. They're preparing the contract and pledge promise right now."

"No problem. We have a fax right here. You call the publisher then I'll go help you get the picture."

They had just put the picture in place when the caterer showed up and everyone went to change.

"Very nice," Brand commented on entering their room and seeing Rachael.

"You think it will do?" She turned letting the skirt flow out from her legs.

"Perfect." He watched her. "Give me a minute to change, and we'll go down together.

"I want to put on some make-up."

Brand was tempted to say she didn't need any, she was already perfect, but after living with a sister, he knew you didn't comment to a woman about her make-up.

A quick shower, a clean pair of pants, a fresh shirt and Brand was ready to go. He smiled when he saw her pacing the floor. "Hey, gorgeous, could I interest you in a handsome escort?"

"I don't know, you volunteering?" She met his playful tone.

"Always." He extended his hand. She placed her hand in it. There was no hesitancy in her coming to him. "No worries."

"I wouldn't say that."

"I would, but it will be my pleasure to take care of you." He kept his kiss brief. "Come on darlin', we have a party to go to, and I want to introduce my beautiful, talented, new wife around."

Rachael found it wasn't really so bad. In fact, she enjoyed herself. The people she met were very nice and friendly, and if anyone was shocked to find out about Brand's sudden marriage, they didn't show it.

She was introduced to several government officials including the governor and a senator of the state. There were a couple of other names and people she recognized from the media. Everyone seemed to think it was interesting that she was a photographer though discounted it until they saw her work displayed for the auction then she had quite a few come back and comment on it. Especially, on her own flare of painting onto the mat.

Brand beamed at her side always right there to support her with his arm around her waist, holding her hand, or some kind of body contact. He touched her continually, but they were honest touches, never fake or forced for show.

"Ready to get something to eat?"

Rachael shivered as his breath brushed her ear when they moved from the couple that they had been talking to. She nodded turning her head so his lips brushed her skin, letting the feel of Brand race through her.

⋘⋙

Brand watched Rachael turn to him. Her face lit with reaction to match his. The energy from just being near her crackled through him, she made him feel alive, vibrant. Her shyness was heartwarming. Her pleasure was exhilarating.

She was having a good time. She innocently charmed all in her wake, and then astonished them when they found out how talented she was. He felt like a proud papa, but his feelings for her were anything but fatherly. Unable to resist, he let his lips trail along her cheek where they lingered for a heart stopping second.

"This better be the new bride." A voice boomed behind them. "If not, you're asking for trouble. Though, trouble like that could be worth it."

Brand turned to introduce Rachael to the man.

"I heard you went to Vegas to pick up some horses from Frome. If this is what you get, maybe I'll have to go check it out."

"Sorry, Bill, she's a one of a kind deal."

"Some men have all the luck."

"I'm thinking so." Brand agreed. "Rachael, this is William Hammond. Bill, Rachael."

"I saw that picture of yours, little lady. Awful good. They say you're a professional photographer. That you do wildlife."

"Yes."

"Do you paint around all of them like that?"

"Usually."

"You don't happen to have some shot of Eagles do you?" Bill Hammond asked.

"Yes, I do," Rachael nodded.

"Hammond Ranch is called Eagle Rest," Brand added, so she knew where the man was going.

"I'd like to see some of your eagles," the man asked in his blunt manner.

"I only have one with me now. I'd be happy to show you, but it's contracted for a calendar. The others will have to wait until I go pick up my belongings to move here."

"I'd sure appreciate it if you'd show me that picture," the man pressed.

"How about now?" Brand suggested.

"My thoughts exactly." He offered his arm. "Ma'am."

"Are you hitting on my wife?" Brand took her other arm.

"If you hadn't found her first and I was twenty years younger, you bet I would, and you wouldn't have stood a chance. In fact, come to think of it, scratch the twenty years. The only thing keeping me from chasing her is you."

"Sorry, I'm not giving her up," Brand came back.

"You'd be a fool if you did. And your mama didn't raise any fools."

After looking at the pictures then promising he could be the first to see the other eagles when she returned with them, they headed back to the party.

"Now how about we get something to eat?" Brand directed her toward the food tables where refreshments were set up to carry guest through the afternoon. "You're going to think I'm trying to starve you."

"I have a feeling you're the one that's hungry."

"How right you are." The look he gave her back turned into a double innuendo. He chuckled when the blush heated her face.

They just reached the table when a tall brunette approached them. "Brand, I've been looking for you," she said, wrapping her arm around his waist, leaning into kiss him as he tried to pull back. "I didn't see you when I arrived. How about taking me to the stable?" The woman continued, not giving him a chance answer. "And show me those new mares of yours." She tried to turn him, but he stepped back.

"Brenda."

"I heard the craziest thing when I got here. You'll just laugh. Tad Hughes tried to convince me you got married."

"That's right," Brand said simply. "Brenda, I'd like you to meet Rachael, my wife." He reached for Rachael pulling her closer. He was afraid after Brenda's little show that she'd be tense. Surprisingly, she wasn't. She curved into his side as natural as she'd been doing all afternoon. Her one arm came around him while her other hand extended.

"Hello," Rachael said.

"Rachael, Brenda lives on the neighboring ranch."

"You're married," Brenda's voice rang with utter disbelief. "That's impossible. You were only gone six days. You ... no, you wouldn't do that. I don't believe it."

"It's true, legally and happily married. When Rachael and I met, I knew it was special."

"You never said you wanted to get married," the woman argued.

"I hadn't thought about it until I met Rachael. It's amazing how fast things change and what becomes important to you."

"Yes, amazing," Brenda repeated. "I presume you're still going to show me your mares."

"Sure, why don't you come over later this week, and I'll introduce you to them."

"We couldn't go now?"

"Sorry, we were just about to get something to eat, and I want to stay close to Rachael," he apologized.

"Well, I'll just join you then." She moved up beside him cutting Rachael out.

Rachael looked past her and Brand shrugged back. At the table things grew even more tense as Brenda refused to acknowledge the others at the table they joined. The others didn't have the same problem probing Rachael about herself, and her and Brand's meeting. By this point, the answers became pretty automatic. It was when Rachael said she was a photographer that she got Brenda's attention.

"Oh, how do you handle it all day getting those little kids to smile? It must get frustrating," Brenda probed.

"I don't take pictures of people. I'm a wildlife photographer, which can be a little frustrating because you can't tell an animal to smile pretty or hold still for the camera. But it's really exciting when you can catch them in action and get a great shot."

"Sounds exciting," Brenda returned dryly. "I guess you're Miss Outdoors then. It'll be quite a change for you to stay home and cook and clean for Brand."

"Not really." Rachael refused to let the woman antagonize her. "Only about four to seven percent of my time is spent out in the field. That means that for every day outdoors, I spend twenty at home in the lab, mounting, detailing and so on. And as for the other, I love to cook and have lots of other hobbies besides. I enjoy sports and riding horses, so I should be able to find things to keep me busy."

"So you ride?"

"Yes, I have my own horse. I use her quite a bit. Some of the places I shot are only accessible on foot or by horse."

"Isn't that scary being so close to animals?" One of the other ladies at the table asked.

"I'm pretty careful and take all the precautions that I can. There have been a couple tense situations, but it's more than likely if the animals know I'm there, they'll just take off."

"What was your most dangerous incident?" the woman's husband asked.

"I was photographing some eagles taking fish right off the lake. They were incredible. I was so involved watching them and getting my shots that I walked up on a grizzly who had been fishing also. I really lucked out because he decided I wasn't a threat and his fish was more appealing, but it was closer than I like to play it. I thought he was going to take me for a minute."

"What did you do?" the woman asked breathless.

"I froze with my finger on the camera, and unbelievably, I got some great close up shots. When he went back to eating, I slowly backed away. I was able to shoot another couple hundred pictures of him and the eagles but at a safe distance."

"Incredible," the man uttered.

"Things don't happen like that often. Most outings are quite boring in a way, but I like the challenge of getting the picture."

"Brand, how are you going to handle her going off into the wilds like that?" Brenda inquired. "Or are you going to make her stop?"

"No way would I ask her to do that. She's too talented. I'll just go with her," he assured. "I already know a few places I plan to take her." He reached out for Rachael's hand. "And if you'll excuse us, I need to take her away now. We're about to start the auction, and we haven't even had a chance to walk through and see if there's anything she would like me to get for her."

He escorted her toward the display area. "Sorry about that," he said once they were away from everyone.

"About what?"

"Brenda. I know she's a little spoiled and can be catty, but honestly, I've never seen her act like that."

"I don't think she liked losing you," Rachael returned simply.

"You got that wrong. There's never been anything between Brenda and me."

"Maybe to you, but I'm not certain about her," Rachael said it more to herself but he heard it.

"You aren't going to get jealous are you?"

"No." Rachael smiled back and on impulse stretched up and kissed him lightly. "But I do think Brenda is."

"I promise there's nothing between us. We've gone to a few horse shows, functions and such but never really as a date. Brenda always has her string of men she toys with. I've never been one of them. It'd be like being with my cousin."

"You might feel that way, but I still don't think she does. That woman is jealous." Rachael could tell Brand didn't believe her but let it drop while they walked through the auction items.

"See anything that takes your fancy?"

"Until I see the house, I'm not certain. I don't even know what the landscaping looks like."

"I'll show you tomorrow. Right now, it's just a meadow. So you can do whatever you like," Brand told her.

"I guess my pick would be the gazebo or the swing if there's a place to put it." She shrugged.

"There's a place. We can sit and watch the stars, and I can steal kisses nice and private." He leaned down to give her a demonstration.

"It isn't very private here."

"So I'll have to try again later."

And he did get the gazebo and the swing plus a lot of lively teasing from the male members of the crowd and a huge cheer from the women. When Rachael tried to tell him he needn't bother, he waved it off.

"I know I can build one myself, but it's all for fun. I'd give the money to the hospital anyway, so would most of the people here. It's just a bonus to get something nice back."

Rachael understood when her picture went for a mind boggling figure, and the owner wholeheartedly agreed to let it be used in the book for the extra donation.

With the auction over, the barbecue began. The food was incredible. Rachael felt comfortable and relaxed until she left the table to get some more food. She hadn't noticed Brenda follow her or come up behind her until she heard the voice.

"You think you have Brand, but you don't. I'm the one who's meant to be with him. I'm the one here for him and the one he always comes back to."

Chapter Thirteen

Rachael didn't get time to comment back before the woman walked away leaving her with a cold feeling of déjà vu.

"What's wrong?" Brand asked, as she returned to the table, picking up the change in her.

"Nothing," she tried to wave it off but it didn't work.

Sliding his arm around her, he leaned close. "Come on, talk to me."

"I don't think you'll believe this, but I was just warned off by Brenda."

"Warned off?"

She nodded. "She said I shouldn't plan on keeping you." When she saw the misunderstanding in his eyes, she decided not to tell him what Brenda said about her having him.

"Well, I tell you, you're not only keeping me, and you'll find me awful hard to get rid of." He let his lips drop to hers.

The familiar taste of him came through the taste of the barbecue on his lips adding to the savor of it.

"Umm, this is good," Brand murmured against her lips as if reading her thoughts.

"Newlyweds." The word came, followed by the clatter of laughter. Breaking apart, Rachael's face burned, Brand looked slightly smug.

"Don't worry, dear." A matronly woman at the table laid a hand on her arm. "It's good to see new love, and

Brand is such a handsome catch. I wouldn't mind stealing a kiss or two from him myself."

"Why, Ester, you never told me." He stood up coming around the table to place a kiss on the woman's cheek.

"Rogue." The woman blushed, as she probably hadn't done in years. "Dear, you are in for a handful of trouble with that scamp."

"I think I agree," Rachael was back to feeling delightfully happy.

Brand stepped behind her laying his hands on her shoulders. "I'd like to agree too since they're about to start the dancing. I requested the first song so I can dance with my wife." He slid a hand down her arm to her hand, feeling her shiver answering the electricity that ran through him as he touched her. "Rachael."

She took his hand letting him lead her away from the table. She didn't notice they were the center of attention. She was focused only on Brand. The music started on cue as they reached the center of the deck reserved for dancing.

Rachael slipped easily into his arms, and as the first time they danced, the surroundings faded away. It was only her and Brand moving with the music as the country singer proclaimed he would do anything to have her stay forever.

Turning, he brought her closer and sighed when her forehead rested against his cheek. She snuggled in to rest against his neck. Her gentle breath teased the skin bared in the V of his collar, raising his already peaked awareness of her.

He let one hand drift down to rest on the curve of her hip while the other lingered over her back before running through her hair, shifting her head so he could find access to her lips which opened in a soft greeting to him.

Brand forced himself to remember where they were, and that they had an audience watching, but it was hard when he was losing his head in the kiss. Gently he broke the kiss running his lips along her temple as she rested her head back down on his shoulder.

"I love dancing with you," she whispered.

"We do pretty well together, don't we?" He gave her a squeeze and pressed another kiss to her temple.

"Better than I knew possible."

He felt the rose petal brush of her lips against his neck.

"You're happy then?"

"Oh, yes. I've had a wonderful day."

"I'm glad. I was concerned it would be too much."

"So was I." She did her little snuggle kitten thing that about blew every circuit in his body.

"Think you could like it here?" He decided to press.

"As long as I'm with you." Her words were so open they took him by surprise. He hardly dared believe they were real and not just what he wanted to hear.

"How do you like it here?"

⋘⋙

Rachael found herself asked almost the same question from the governor's wife a few minutes later, after the governor asked to talk to Brand in private for a moment.

"I like it a lot. The Morgans are wonderful."

"So you don't think you'll have a hard time leaving your home and moving here?"

"No, this is where Brand is." Knowing what she said was true. Where Brand was, was all that was important.

"What a wonderful answer. There aren't many today who could do that," the woman said sadly.

"My work doesn't really require me to live in any one place. Brand's does."

"Well, I still think it's a wonderful attitude. I'm impressed you feel like you're not giving up too much."

"I think I'm getting much more than I'm giving up." She smiled back politely.

As soon as the woman moved on Dallas stepped up.

The day had been so busy, it was the first time she'd been alone with Brand's brother.

"You know I was concerned there for a while," Dallas started. "What it would do to Brand when you took off? What people would think and all? But I guess I got that part all wrong. I should have realized it's as you said. You're getting much more by staying, than leaving and having him look like a stooge."

"Excuse me." Rachael couldn't believe what she'd heard.

"It worked out rather nice for you, didn't it? You got the money and the right contacts for your photos. The one for charity was a good touch, though it's paying off. Maybe that's where I made my mistake."

Rachael felt as if ice was forming in her veins, but his words kept coming. She tried to fight back. "I don't need his money, and I have my own contacts, I'm here …"

"I know why you're here." He cut her off. "You don't fool me, and you can take your money and stuff it, but I'm warning you. Don't hurt him or I'll get even." The threat was unmistakable enough to send shivers through her.

She shook her head in denial. "I would never hurt him."

"Because you love him."

"Yes!"

"That's conveniently fast."

"It was fast, but not convenient and it doesn't mean it's not right. Brand and I are aware our relationship started off rather … unorthodox, but we're trying to give it a chance. Can't you give me one, too?" Rachael found herself pleading. "Please, just give me a chance. I have no desire to use him." She felt the tears flood back in her eyes but refused to let them flow.

"You'd sign a prenuptial agreement?" he challenged.

"We're already married, but if it would help, I'll sign it."

He simply nodded and, without another comment, walked away.

Rachael felt like crying. Maybe it was all a dream. Maybe she wasn't meant to be with Brand and fit in his world and family. Turning from the party, she wandered away until the only light was from the stars. It was so beautiful here. But maybe like the stars, it was out of reach.

Tears finally trickled free. She couldn't rip apart Brand's family, and Dallas certainly didn't want her there. His mother had tried to make her feel welcome, and so had his sister. Rachael tried again to push back the tears. Maybe all it would take was time for Dallas to accept her. She would sign his papers. It didn't matter to her. She only wanted to stay with Brand.

She had made a success of running away from people, now it was time to see what she could do if she stayed and confronted them. Not tonight though, she sighed wearily, leaning back against a tree. Tonight she had enough. She was drained. Letting her eyes drift closed she listened to the distant music.

Rachael wasn't sure what alarmed her, but her eyes flew open, and she pulled away from the tree. "Hello." Her voice got lost in the shadows her eyes searched. She hadn't realized she had come so far from the house. Suddenly, she felt very uneasy, alone and unprotected, which was silly because how often she went into the woods alone without feeling that way and for her to be just yards from hundreds of people. She shook it off.

"Hello?" she said again taking a step forward. There was no answer, but her skin crawled. Someone was there, watching. She could feel them. She had relied on her instinct enough to know to trust it. Another shudder went through her and she turned, heading for the house.

As she drew near, she saw Brand about the same time he saw her and headed her way. "There you are. I couldn't find you."

"I went for a walk," she said, hoping it wasn't obvious that she had been crying.

"I thought you might like to dance again. It's getting late."

"I'd love to dance." Nothing sounded better to her than to being in his arms.

She followed him to the dance floor, stepping to him when he opened his arms for her. Snuggling close, she dropped her head to his shoulder, resting one hand on his chest. She felt his muscle contract under her hand and stroked it unconsciously. Letting her eyes drift closed, just enjoying the feel of his arms.

Brand knew something had upset her. He could feel the tension leave her body as she relaxed into him. The hand which rested on his chest made small caresses that had the opposite effect on him.

"Tired?" His voice picked up a gravelly tone. When she nodded, her cheek rubbed against his chest making him swallow a groan. "You could go up to bed if you want. People are leaving, and no one would mind if you cut out."

This time she shook her head. "I want to stay with you." Her words about melted him on the spot. The next were worse. "Please, hold me."

"Rachael, are you all right?"

There was another small nod against his chest. "Just hold me."

The song ended and the next began. Brand didn't break his hold. He felt the shiver run through her as he stroked her back, and she pressed closer. When he brought a hand up over her shoulder to cup her cheek, she tilted her face with the motion ready to accept his kiss and give back her own. Brand's body jumped from warm to steaming in a second. He tried to shift back but Rachael pressed closer, caressing her lips against his neck.

"Rachael, I need to let you go."

"No, please."

Her objection almost got the better of him. "If I don't, sweetheart, I'm going to take you upstairs and make love to you."

"Yes, please." Her words froze him.

"Rachael?" He cleared his throat.

She lifted her head, looking into his eyes. There was no missing the desire, which gave her courage. "I want to make love with you. I want you to make me yours again, this time forever." Rachael decided to take his mother's advice and lay it all in the open. "I love you."

That was all Brand needed to hear. Taking her hand, he led her to the stairway up to the balcony away from the people. He paused at the French doors. Cupping her face in his hands, he tilted her up so that even in the party lights sparkling like a myriad of little fireflies below, he could still see her eyes. "Are you sure about this?"

"I've never been surer of anything in my life. I want to make love with you."

With a growl, he kissed her. Lifting his head, he looked at her. "I love you." The words were deep and deliberate. "From this moment you are mine." He lifted her into his arms and carried her inside.

◌ℨ৪০

A feeling of rightness drifted over Rachael along with a work roughened hand as she stretched herself awake. The heeded masculine smell that surrounded her was as soothing and exciting as the lips nuzzling her neck and cheek.

The sigh that snuck out of her was deep and drawn out and answered by a chuckle which shocked her slightly. "Come on, sleepyhead." The lips teased her again. Opening her eyes, there was no panic waking up beside Brand, not after making love the better part of the night.

"Good morning." His voice was a gravelly tone she now recognizes as desire.

"The best." She stretched feeling him pressed all along her.

"Ummm." He tightened his arm around her. "You're awfully nice to wake up with." He kissed her lightly.

"You're awfully nice to sleep with," she returned with a kiss of her own.

"I don't think much of what we did in this bed last night can be qualified as sleep, but boy, do I feel good." He trailed his lips along her cheek.

"Me, too." She turned to catch his mouth.

He lifted his head, suddenly serious. "Are you all right?" Brand brushed back her hair then lifted a strand letting it slide through his fingers.

She nodded touching her lips to his fingers. "I've never felt this wonderful before."

"I'm going to have to see you keep feeling this way." He came back for the kiss that grew into more.

 C380

Everyone was done with breakfast and scattered when they finally came down. Brand was still humming the song she had first fallen to sleep with the night before. She found herself singing along with him, about never wanting to miss a thing.

"I didn't know you sang." He wrapped his arm around her waist from behind as she poured herself some juice.

"I don't really. I just sing with the radio and while I work around the house."

"In the shower?" His question was answered when her cheeks pinkened. "I missed that this morning." He kissed her letting her know he didn't miss much else. "I'll have to catch that later."

"We'll see."

"Brand, Rachael." His mother came into the room. "I thought you took off with everyone else."

"We're having a slow morning, but I was just about to take Rachael for a ride to show her around."

"That ought to be nice."

"Where's everyone else?" he asked.

"Richard, Beth and the boys had to get back. Dallas had to go to Phoenix for a meeting. He said he would be back in a couple days. Candy ran into town." Emily ticked off the list.

"How did the fundraiser do?" Rachael asked.

"Wonderful, we exceeded my goal by quite a ways. Thank you. I had a lot of comments on your picture by the way. We'll have to have a showing for you. When will you be going for your things?"

Rachael looked to Brand. "We haven't talked about that yet."

"I need to be around for a couple days and have an auction to attend in a couple weeks, but I can go any time after that, just name the date," Brand said.

"I don't know maybe in three weeks. There's a lot to do. I guess I'll have to sell my house. I hadn't thought much about it." She felt a heavy weight on her heart.

"If you want, it can wait. You don't have to decide now," Brand said, picking up her attitude change. "And we can sit down later and decide the rest. There's no hurry."

She smiled.

"You just reminded me. If you give me a moment, I have to make a phone call."

"Sure, I'll start breakfast."

"Thanks." He kissed her cheek.

His mother waited until he left the room before turning to her. "Well, I take it you told him how you feel."

"Is it that obvious?"

"Yes. Even if I didn't see you disappear last night and you didn't look well loved. My son is walking around like one, very happy man. Not that he wasn't yesterday, but the tension in him is gone."

"I didn't know it was so bad."

"That he was walking around looking at his wife like he wanted to devour her."

Rachael laughed.

"Don't laugh, she's right."

Rachael jumped, looking guilty over at Brand. "We were talking about you," she stated the obvious.

"So I heard. Do I get to join in?"

"Of course," his mother said. "It's much more fun to talk about you in front of your face. That way I can see the reactions. Rachael was concerned yesterday how to tell you she loved you. I was just saying it looked like it turned out fine."

"Very." He moved behind Rachael pressing a kiss to her neck, taking the egg from her hand, breaking it into the pan.

"As much as I enjoy talking about you, I have to run myself. I have a meeting at the children's hospital. The auction items have all been moved into storage. Martha can see to any pick-ups on them today. Brand, can you see to the chairs and tables this afternoon? Dallas didn't have time before he left."

"Sure," he agreed as his mother gave him a kiss on the cheek.

"Thanks." She gave Rachael a hug and was out the door.

"Your mother is great."

"Yeah, I'm pretty lucky. You had a nice talk with her?"

"She's easy to talk to." Rachael shifted a little uneasy. "Actually," Rachael's guilty look remained, "I didn't tell you yet." She swallowed. "I told your mother what happened."

"It's all right," he assured as he slipped his arm around her.

Rachael couldn't believe how natural it seemed to slide her own arms around his waist but her voice failed her when she went to explain. "I …"

"You needed someone to talk to," he finished for her. "I'm glad you felt you could talk to my mother."

"It was what I needed with everything that happened. I wasn't sure how to tell you I loved you."

"Then I have a lot to thank my mother for. Since there's nothing to worry about, now, let's eat."

"You really don't mind? I know we weren't going to tell anyone."

"Rachael." Brand stopped her, reaching out to cup her chin, turning her to look at him. "I understand. You needed to talk to another female. I might have told my mother sooner or later. I'm just glad you felt you could turn to her," he said sincerely.

"It felt good to have someone to cry to, to give me a hug." She was embarrassed. "I mean it's different then when … you hug me."

"I hope so."

"I'm not explaining myself very well am I?"

"You're doing quite well, and I'm glad you don't see my hugs like my mother's. It wouldn't do any good for my ego."

"You and your ego again."

"Hey, men are fragile. We take a lot of care."

"I'd say. Now are we going to eat so you can show me this beautiful ranch you have here," she said firmly.

"Yes, ma'am."

Chapter Fourteen

Sugar Baby was as sweet as her name and the color of caramel. She had a nice easy gallop, and Rachael made fast friends with her. Torrent, the horse Brand rode, was one of his stallions. His black coat was marbled with gray making him look like a stormy night. He was big, beautiful and spirited, but under Brand's firm hand, performed beautifully.

Rachael stopped Sugar just to watch the man and the horse canter across the field. Their motions were as in sync as dancers to music. The horse's step precise, the man so tall and perfect in the saddle, she ran through a couple dozen shots before Brand realized she wasn't with him. She got more shots as he came racing back.

"I thought you took pictures of wildlife?"

"I do," she said impishly.

"Are you suggesting that Torrent is wild or that I am?"

"I'm not telling." She urged Sugar forward. "Are we going to follow the fence this way?"

"Actually, I need to check the fence in another section. John said it was down when I talked to him. He dropped the things off I'll need to fix it, when he headed to the next section so we could ride. We're going to head west now. It's just there by the grove of trees and creek. Over there is the Bar B." He pointed in the direction

"The Barbie?" She laughed.

"No. Bar B Ranch, Brenda's family ranch. Her father's name is Bart and his father was Brent. That's where the original B came from. All first names start with B."

"So you fit in, in her eyes," she said thoughtfully.

"Now, don't start that."

She caught his wicked look, but he just changed the subject. "If you follow the fence, it goes to the highway. It's a nice ride whenever you want to go, sheltered by trees to give plenty of shade. The trees were planted by my great-great grandfather. They're about a hundred and forty years old."

"It sure makes it pretty."

"Wait until fall and you see the colors. He came from New England, and he missed the leaves changing. That's why he planted them. Most of what's native to this area is pine and scrub. There are a few others, but nothing compared to what he was used to. Now we have people drive out here each fall just to see the leaves."

"It sounds like it means as much to you as it did to him." Her comment brought on a grin.

"Yeah, it does. This is where I always ride when I have time just to relax. I was going to wait and show you this after I'd fixed the fence but come on." He turned Torrent and headed off on a slow gallop, letting her follow.

They came to the dirt road they crossed a couple minutes earlier then followed it about three hundred yards through the trees. Rachael saw the structure as the trees opened into a clearing. It was still at the framing stage, but she could see its outline. The door was in but the windows hadn't been set yet. It was a large house, nowhere near the size of the main house, but big enough to give a family plenty of room to grow.

"I'm sorry it's not finished, but I hadn't planned on meeting you." He swung off his horse and came around lifting his arms for her. "Let me show you our home."

Rachael placed her hands on his shoulders, and he lifted her down. Keeping his eyes locked on hers until her feet touched the ground. Then he turned her not breaking contact.

"You can see where the garage is. There'll be a wraparound porch all the way to the patio in back. I took the idea from my grandfather." Leading her to the house, he scooped her up in his arms, carrying her over the threshold.

"Tradition, hmm." She kissed him.

"You got it. Besides I like having you in my arms. The formal dining and living room are here on this side from there to there. The kitchen is behind the dining. The laundry and mud room off it, with an entry to the garage. There's a room for a housekeeper, but I thought we could change it into a studio and workroom for you, if you'd like. It's a large room so we can shift the wall off the bathroom for a darkroom or what you need. You'd still have plenty of room with lots of natural light to paint by, or I can build you a separate studio out back."

"Actually this sounds great. I don't need a lot of room. At home, I just converted a small spare bedroom."

"I want you to have it how you always wanted it." He made it clear what she asked for, he'd do. "The breakfast nook juts out and has a bay window, then there's a large family room and my den. Upstairs there will be five bedrooms."

"Oh, which one will be mine?"

"The one with the master bath, and a tub big enough for two and." He dropped his voice. "Me."

"And who were you planning to share that tub for two with before I came along?"

"I just changed it. It was just a plain jetted tub."

"Sure it will fit?"

"I'm sure, even if I have to knock down the wall, it'll fit."

Rachael couldn't keep in her laughter. The next instant she was caught tight against him, with his mouth catching her laughter. With a sigh Rachael gave herself over to him.

"Do you … know," he said between kisses. "How much … I wish, the tub was in … there now. I'm tempted to take you upstairs and make love to you on those bare boards that will be our bedroom."

"So what's stopping you?" she challenged back.

"You could get a sliver."

"All good things are worth the risk."

With a growl, he swung her back into his arms and headed up the staircase, staying close to the wall away from the missing railing.

"You promise to take care of any slivers."

"Oh, I promise, tender, loving, care and I'll even kiss it better."

⚜

Rachael lay back in the grass on Brand's shirt watching his muscles strain. She wished she hadn't just filled her memory card. She thought of clearing some memory but then she didn't need a picture to know how Brand looked. It was engraved in her mind. All she had to do was close her eyes to see him, on his horse, under the tree where he laid as they ate lunch, in the house that they would share. The sun played on his muscles as he worked to repair the fence.

"Hey, sleepyhead." The soft petal of a wildflower tickled her cheek. "I must really be wearing you out."

Rachael opened her eyes to find him stretched out beside her.

"You're sounding a little smug there."

"A man likes to know his powers are appreciated."

"Oh, it is." She slipped her arms up around his neck, easily pulling him down to her kiss.

"You know we're a little in the open here."

"I've never made love in the outdoors."

"Neither have I." He kissed her, drinking deep as her hands roamed over the muscles of his sun-heated back. "I've created a monster," he growled.

"What are you going to do about it?"

"Enjoy and take very good care of it for a long time."

෫෨෧෭

Rachael woke up alone in bed. Feeling the spot next to her, the sheets were cool. She remembered Brand kissing her good-bye and telling her to go back to sleep but was surprised she did. Maybe it was the change of altitude, the drier climate, or Brand was wearing her out. But she was just so sleepy.

After being at the ranch for a week, she knew her way around. It wasn't hard to find Brand at the stables. "Good morning."

He came out of the stall to meet her. "You okay?" he asked, his arm stealing around her.

"I'm fine, just so tired. Thanks for letting me sleep. I needed it."

"You're welcome." He pulled his hand from his leatherwork glove to trace his finger down her cheek then followed it for a kiss.

"Can I help?" she asked, trying to keep her heart calm.

"Just finished up, I was about to head up to the house. I have some paperwork to get done, then I was going to wake you. I called for a doctor appointment. They had a cancellation this afternoon so they can see us both. I'll be glad to get these stitches out of my arm. I was tempted to do it myself this morning. Rachael, are you okay?" He noticed her pale face.

"Yeah, just going to the doctor makes me nervous."

"Don't worry you'll like Dr. Grayson. He's an older doctor, balding on top, a real kind grandfatherly type. There's nothing to worry about."

"I know but that doesn't make it easier. I'm not sure what to think either way. Pregnant or not?"

"Do you think you're pregnant?"

"I haven't had any morning sickness, but I don't know if I should yet. When's our appointment?"

"Two, so we ought to go catch lunch. I need to change."

"I'll make lunch while you change and then we can leave. There are a few things I need to get, if you don't mind."

"Not at all. Shopping it is."

ೞ೩೪

Rachael was so tense by the time Brand turned into the medical complex if she was a bow, she would snap. He'd been right not to tell her about the appointment until about time. She was almost trembling with fear. Her actions worried him since they moved past the point of whether or not she was pregnant making a difference if they stayed together.

He didn't want her to worry. He wondered if she really did want a baby even though she had once said she hoped there was one. It would change her life even more than being married to him.

Physically, she wouldn't be able to go out in the outdoors the way she did. After the baby was born, she would be tied down. But if there wasn't a baby, well, he didn't want to think about that.

Selfishly, he wanted a child. The thought of a part of him growing in her thrilled him like he couldn't believe. Funny how fast things changed. A month ago he hadn't thought of being married or expecting a family even though he knew he wanted one someday. Now, he wanted Rachael and a baby more than anything.

He pulled into a parking place and came around to help her out. Her hand was like ice and trembled as he took it. "It's all right." He gave her a warm smile meant to build her confidence.

"I know, I just can't help being nervous. I feel like I'm on a precipice, and I'm not sure which way's the cliff."

"Will it help you if I promise to catch you?"

"I know you will. I've just never felt this unsteady before."

"I'm sorry, sweetheart."

"It's not your fault, but I could use a hug if we have time."

"There's always time for that." He wrapped his arms around her. Her head dropped to his shoulder. She snuggled against him with a sigh.

He rubbed his hands over her back, knowing her trembling wasn't from desire. She felt so small against him, fragile. He loved the feel usually, now he wondered how he could make her feel stronger.

When she took a large breath and pulled back, he let her go, keeping a hold of her hand. "Okay?"

"Yes, thanks."

"Anytime." He placed a kiss on her forehead.

The receptionist took their names, and they found a seat until she called them back. "Mrs. Morgan, we don't have a chart on you, if you could just fill out these papers." She handed her a clipboard, "and I need your insurance information." Rachael reached for her purse but Brand stopped her.

"I've already put her on my insurance."

"You did?" Rachael was surprised.

"Right after we left Mitch's office." He turned back to the receptionist. "I'll fill that out. Her new insurance card hasn't gotten here yet."

Five minutes later, Brand was at the desk when the nurse called her. "You go. I'll be right there." He motioned to her.

They took her weight and blood pressure, then giving her a tissue gown told her the doctor would be with her in a minute. Rachael changed then climbed up on the examination table, feeling totally exposed wearing just a little bit of paper. She was clenching her hands and studying the posters on the walls, when there was a light tap on the door. She expected Brand to enter; instead, it was an older, average height man, who was balding. The nurse followed him into the room.

"Hello there, I'm Dr. Grayson."

"Rachael Morgan."

"Any relation to Emily?" he asked.

"She's my new mother-in-law. I just married Brand."

"I wondered. I was called in on the afternoon of the auction but I heard the news. I admit it was a surprise."

"I'd say Brand and I were the most surprised."

"Are you getting along?" he pried.

"Oh yes, I didn't mean it like that. It was just that neither Brand nor I were planning on marrying now." She stopped to take a deep breath. "I'm sorry, I'm nervous. I figured Brand would be in with me."

"I'll have the nurse see what's keeping him." He nodded to the nurse and the woman left.

"While your nurse is looking for Brand, I have a request. There is some information I want to keep out of my records so only you know."

"If it's a risk factor."

"It isn't, it's something that happened to Brand and I. But we don't want it known. Maybe if you read this, you'll understand." She handed him the spare copy of Mitch's report.

It only took a couple seconds for him to understand what she was talking about and he nodded. There was another knock on the door. This time it was Brand that entered.

"I see Rachael gave you the report." Brand noticed the papers in the doctor's hand as they exchanged greetings.

"Yes, we can skip putting this in your file but I'd like to run a blood test. Though there should be no aftereffects of the drug."

"That's what Dr. Adams told us," Brand said moving over to Rachael.

"Well, why don't we get those blood tests and then we can get those stitches out, and do the exam."

Brand wasn't concerned about the newly healing scare on his arm. Rachael hadn't said a word after they drew blood. She held tight to his opposite hand while he leaned back against the examination table as the stitches were removed.

Now that they were finished Brand's hold on her tightened.

"All right, Rachael, your turn." Dr. Grayson said stepping to the sink.

"Can Brand stay in the room?" Her voice quivered.

"Certainly." He turned back. "Whatever you want, Brand, if you would stand by her head. Rachael, I need you to lay back and put your feet in the stirrups."

She complied then flinched and tightened. Her lip caught between her teeth.

"Relax, Rachael, I know this isn't comfortable," the doctor said.

"Well, anything you want to talk about?" Brand tried to break her tension, and it worked as a laugh escaped her.

"I don't know. The weather's nice."

"Maybe we can go for a picnic," he suggested more serious than joking.

"I'm for that. Can we leave now?"

"I don't know. Dr. Grayson, can you join us?" Brand asked.

"I don't think I was included in that invitation, and I'm afraid I'll have to hold you up just a few minutes more, just about done here," he said setting back.

"Dr. Grayson?" Rachael questioned.

"Let's wait for the blood test for confirmation," he answered gently.

"But what do you think?" she prodded.

"Easy." Brand stroked her fingers, feeling his own desire to press.

"I'm trying," she said, coming close to tears. "If I just knew one way or the other."

"It will only be a couple minutes more." The doctor tried to console. "Why don't you get dressed, and we should know by the time you're finished. I'll go get the results myself."

Reluctantly, she nodded as he stepped from the room.

"Can you turn around?" Her request surprised him, but Brand turned.

"I think it's a little too late to hide anything from me," he teased with a smile on his face. Especially, since he was facing the mirror giving him a complete view of her.

"I know but this feels so embarrassing sitting here like this."

"I don't know. It could be advantageous. Think how easy it would be for me to tear it off you and have my wicked way. Maybe I should ask Doc if I can get a few of those." He pretended to be thoughtful.

"They're not very flattering."

"Yeah, but I have a great memory of what's hidden underneath." He didn't fight the huskiness from his voice. "I have a very sexy wife."

"I'm dressed."

"Dang, I was thinking of coming to help." He turned and reached for her, taking her in his arms, bending her backwards. His kiss was interrupted by the knock on the door, and Dr. Grayson stepped in. Brand felt Rachael's body tighten as did his own as they waited for what was to be said.

"Dr. Grayson?" Rachael managed to get out.

"Well, it's confirmed."

"I'm …" Rachael's voice faltered.

"You're pregnant." The doctor nodded.

"I'm … a baby." One hand released Brand's and dropped to her abdomen. "We're going to–"

"Brand, you better boost her back up on the table," Grayson suggested, then continued as Brand did. "I know what happened, but from what she said, I thought this may be a case of congratulations."

"It is," Brand assured him, not feeling too reassured himself. "She gets this way when she's blown over."

"I'm sorry." What they were saying penetrated her mind. "Mitch said it was possible but it didn't seem. I mean, how many women get pregnant their very first time."

"It only takes once." The doctor smiled.

"I know but, oh my." She looked to Brand. "We're going to have a baby."

"Yes."

"Is that okay?" She looked to him expectantly as she waited for his answer, it wasn't a long wait.

"It's more than okay, it's wonderful."

Tears flooded her eyes. "You really do want the baby?"

"I do and I want its mother, too."

"Oh." Her arms went around him. She buried herself in his chest and cried.

Feeling a little helpless, he looked to the older man, who answered his unasked question.

"It's okay, it was the right answer. Congratulations."

"Thanks."

"I'll leave you two alone. Use the room as long as you need. I'll leave a prescription for pre-natal vitamins and some literature at the front desk. I'll need to see her again in six weeks. Oh and when she settles down, she'll want to know that there should be no risk to the baby from the drug given her. It would have been out of her system before the fertilized egg attached to her uterus. So everything should be just fine."

"Thanks."

"Thank you." Rachael's whisper echoed Brand's.

"You're welcome." Dr. Grayson patted her shoulder when she lifted her head. "See you in six weeks and get plenty of rest."

Left alone, Brand cupped her cheek in his palm. "Is everything all right?"

She nodded. The hand resting on her stomach stoked it gently. "It's just hard to believe. A baby, me. I look at you and think I must be dreaming we're married. It's so amazing to think we made love, and we made a baby. I just can't believe it's real."

"It's real. I promise it's not a dream. How about we go home now and I show you, how real it all is?"

"I thought we were going on a picnic."

"Do you mind if it's in the middle of our bed?" He pulled her up close to kiss her soundly, as the thought hit him. "Or we could grab a couple sleeping bags, and we can spend the night under the stars?"

"Could we?" She let out excited.

"I'll call Martha and see if she can get us some food put together. I know just the place to take you. Make sure to bring your camera."

Chapter Fifteen

When they pulled up to the house, a new red sports car was parked in the drive. It was unfamiliar to Rachael, but the woman waiting on the porch wasn't. Brenda met Brand as he was coming around the front of the truck.

"Hello," he greeted moving past Brenda to open the door for Rachael, regaining the hold on her hand he'd kept for the most part since leaving the examination room. "What brings you by today?"

"I thought that maybe you'd show me those mares. I've been over several times but you've been busy." She glanced Rachael's way.

"Sorry. I can't today. Rachael and I are just getting ready to go camping. Why don't I call John, and he can show them to you?" Brand suggested.

"Don't bother. I can come back another time."

"No need, it's no bother. I'm sure he won't mind."

"Surely you can take a minute. Rachael won't mind." The woman looked to her, challengingly, leaving no way for her to object without looking bad, but Brand answered first.

"You're right, Rachael wouldn't mind, and she'd prepare everything herself, but I'd mind. I want to be with my wife, and I've decided the only way to get her alone is to kidnap her and take her away. So if you'll excuse us." He scooped Rachael into his arms, cradling her to his chest. Rachael gasped, throwing her arms around his neck then laughed.

He was watching Rachael so close he totally forgot the other woman was there. "Oh sorry." He almost bumped Rachael's feet into her. "John should be down at the stables."

"No, that's okay. I'll come back." Brenda turned with a jerk.

Rachael felt a stab of pity as she watched the woman over Brand's shoulder. He really had no idea she looked at him with more than friendship. The flashy red car spit gravel as it went over the edge of the pavement before it was corrected in its hurried flight to leave.

ભ≪ু

Rachael lay in Brand's arms looking at the sky from in the sleeping bags they had zipped together into one. "Have you ever seen anything so beautiful?"

"Every time I look into your eyes," he said softly, brushing his hand through her hair spreading it over his chest.

"Oh," she pushed herself up leaning over him. "What a beautiful thing to say. You're getting good at that."

"I mean it." He slid his hands up to pull her head down to him. "Have I told you? You have a wonderfully kissable mouth."

"No." The word came out a whisper.

"You do, I like kissing it and I like camping with you."

"I always liked camping but now I think I love it." She tipped her head, eager to receive his kiss. A short time later, she was lying on his chest. His fingers traced lazily along her back.

"Are you all right?" His words did nothing to pull her out of her contentment.

"Wonderful." She pressed her lips to his chest while she raised her hand to caress along his chin.

"It's still hard to believe a baby is growing here." His hand brushed her stomach then settled over it.

"I know."

"Are you still nervous?"

"Not like I was. Now it's more excitement and awe. I just don't know what to expect. I haven't gotten very far on reading the literature Dr. Grayson gave me. I'm still on the part on how the baby is made."

"I think you can skip that part. We seemed to have gotten past that without help."

She gave his chest a light smack. "I don't mean making love. I mean, if you think about the odds of everything being right that first time, it's really amazing."

"A miracle is how I'm counting it and will every day of my life."

"You are definitely getting good at saying the right thing." She smiled down before giving him a heated kiss.

"Like saying I love you." He kissed her in return.

"I love you, too."

"It's a good thing we're in agreement."

03☙

The sun was just lighting the valley when Rachael awoke. She could feel Brand's warm breath on her neck and his arm around her waist. From where they lay, she could see out over the valley. A small lake sat at the bottom with the doe and two fawns by the water's edge.

She was reaching over her head for her backpack when Rachael caught sight of the trophy size buck, his horns still in velvet, stepping out of the trees. Carefully, she brought the camera out and focused the telephoto lens on the buck then clicked a half a dozen shots before moving back to the doe and fawns.

She felt Brand's hand caress down over her back and almost missed the last shot. "You knew they'd be here," she whispered.

"I hoped. They're around here quite a bit." He brushed kisses on her shoulder.

"It's incredible." She reached for her other camera. "This is a perfect spot, but I'd like to move to another location for a different angle, but I'm afraid I'll scare them if I try to get dressed."

"I'll watch for anyone to come if you want to go streaking across the meadow," he whispered playfully, nipping her ear lobe.

"I appreciate it." Leaning over him she grabbed his shirt and pulled it on. Paying more attention to the deer than what she was doing with her hands. The deer were still unconcerned when she slipped from the warm sleeping bag and into her own jeans. She didn't bother with socks as she pulled on her shoes.

Brand watched as she took both cameras, hooked one around her neck, the other in her hand ready to shoot. Making almost no noise, she crept forward, staying low to the ground. After about a hundred yards, she stopped and took several pictures before moving on. She disappeared behind some rocks. When he caught sight of her again, she was only a few feet from the water. He couldn't believe how she moved, like cat hunting its prey.

He watched the buck lift its head and scan the area a minute and realized she was downwind from it. Still after a minute more, he trotted away. The doe remained where it was unconcerned or unaware of Rachael's presence.

Brand could see Rachael shift her attention but not at what she was looking at. She switched cameras. After a few more minutes, she headed back up the hill toward him.

"It's chilly this morning," she gasped reaching him, placing her cameras back in the pack.

"Why don't you get back in here and I'll warm you up," Brand invited.

"I'll warn you I'm cold." Sitting on the top of the sleeping bag, she slid off her shoes, damp from the dew, then her jeans before sliding back into the sleeping bag.

"I'm going to want that shirt back." He reached for the hem.

"Somehow, I thought you might."

"Did you get some good pictures?"

"I think so. There's also some ducks with babies down on the water in the grass. This one was so funny because he kept going the wrong way, and his mother had to keep calling him back, and he'd do this little scurry run across the water thing because he couldn't fly yet. The fawns were so cute together too. Brand, do twins run in your family?"

"Not that I know of, how about yours?"

"Same. I was just thinking that it would be a lot to handle. I kind of hope just one at a time, I mean if it's twins it would be fine."

"Hey, it's all right by me to do them one at a time. I get the fun part. You do all the work." He smiled with a gleam in his eyes.

"You're going to have to put up with me," she said sternly.

"With pleasure."

⟡

Rachael felt more like she was going into hibernation than she was pregnant. She figured Brand had left their room almost two hours earlier, leaving her asleep. Food was the foremost thing on her mind until she approached the kitchen and smelled the fish Martha was preparing for lunch.

Nausea hit her so fast she hardly made it to the hall bathroom. Tears filled her eyes by the time she was able to make it to her feet and the sink. Her body trembled, but her stomach began to settle. Making it out of the bathroom, she headed to the patio instead of the kitchen. She collapsed back in a chair closing her eyes, letting the fresh air revive her.

"Rachael, I didn't know you were out here. I thought you were still upstairs," Martha greeted her.

"I decided some fresh air before breakfast."

"Would you like me to bring you something out here?" the woman volunteered.

"That's not necessary. I'll come in, in a moment," Rachael reassured her.

"You just stay here. It's no problem at all. I was just bringing out Dallas some breakfast." The woman waved her down.

"I didn't know he was back."

"He got in late last night." She just finished saying, when Brand's brother stepped onto the patio carrying a glass of juice.

The sardonic smile he gave her in greeting didn't suggest his feelings toward her softened any.

"What would you like?" Martha drew back her attention.

"Oh, just a couple pieces of toast."

The housekeeper frowned. "Let's add a small bowl of cereal to that."

"Fine, thank you." She glanced at Dallas.

He made her nervous. Though his looks were similar to Brand's and they were both the same height, whatever drew her to Brand was missing in Dallas.

"Did you have a good trip?" She stammered over the words. Cursing herself for letting him bring out the shyness she fought so hard to conquer.

"Yes, it went quite well. The negotiation went just as I wanted."

She nodded trying to think of something else to say.

"And how has your stay here gone? It's been what twelve days, thirteen."

"Thirteen. It's been nice. Brand has taken me riding several times, and we went camping the other night. I got to shoot a lot of photos. I can't print them yet, not until I get my things." Rachael flinched knowing she was doing her habit of talking about photography when she was nervous.

Gratefully, Martha brought out breakfast just then.

She had finished most of a piece of toast when Dallas spoke again. "So you are moving here?"

"Yes."

"And when will that be?"

"The end of next week is the plan. It will take several days to get things ready then Brand is going to bring the horse trailer for the stuff I'm bringing back."

"You have it all worked out."

"I think so."

They were quiet while she finished her toast. Her stomach had settled enough that she started on her cereal.

"Does that include trying to convince Brand that the baby you're carrying is his?"

Rachael dropped the spoon. "What?" She felt sick again.

"I heard you. You're having morning sickness," he stated like it was a plague.

"Yes."

"And you're going to try to tell me that it's Brand's."

"It is Brand's." Her voice quivered, and she felt a chill run through her.

"It's been what two–three weeks, and you expect him to believe it is his. You're going to say it was conceived the first night." He sneered.

"It was," she gasped out and then blushed at her response.

"Is that what you used to get him to marry you? I knew it had to be something. You have him so tied up he can't see straight."

"No, that's not true," Rachael cried.

"Isn't it? You really think you can keep Brand fooled that the baby's his? What happens if the baby's father comes back? Are you going to go with him or are you going to stay where the money is?"

"Brand is the father of the baby," she cried out again desperate for him to believe her.

"Dallas!" Brand's voice boomed as he strode across the patio. "What's going on?"

"We were just having an informative discussion. Did you know your wife," he said it as if it was a swear word, "was pregnant?"

"Yes, I was with her when we found out for sure."

"And you really believe that it's yours. Come on, you've never been gullible enough to let a pretty face cloud your judgment." Dallas didn't hide his feelings.

"Careful," Brand threatened, clearly fighting his temper.

"It's only been couple weeks. How can you be so certain?"

"Because she was a virgin the first night we made love," he shouted back

"Yeah, right. You can believe that of a woman that looks like that," Dallas challenged back.

"I don't believe, I know. There are certain things that are hard to miss even drugged and that is one of them." Too late Brand realized what he'd blurted out and how it sounded. He shifted his attention to Rachael. She stood on the other side of the table. Her face was deathly pale. The hurt in her eyes cut deep.

"Rachael." He stepped toward her, reaching out.

She shook her head backing away, bumping into the chair. "I think I'd like to go lie down. I don't feel so well." Her voice was dull.

"Rachael." Brand took another step only to stop when she shook her head again.

"I ... I need to be alone." She turned and fled.

"Brand?" Dallas started behind him, as Brand watched her disappear.

"Shut up, Dallas, you've done enough damage."

"What did you mean? Was she really?" Dallas lowered his voice.

"You really want to know. All right, I'll tell you. Someone slipped a date rape drug in both our drinks. Whether it was Rachael's old-fashioned dream or fate, we ended up married first. And do you know who the lucky one is? I could have ended up in jail on rape charges. Believe me the police wanted to, but Rachael never doubted me. She's special and I love her. We're trying to make this work and we were doing pretty good until just now. I have a feeling it's going to take a lot of damage control before she lets me near her again."

"I'm sorry, I didn't know."

"You didn't need to know. Trust me, I'm not a kid."

"I just didn't want to see you torn up like I was," Dallas tried to explain.

"I know, but every woman is not like Georgia."

"I know."

"I don't think you do. If you walk around thinking the worst of women, you're going to lose any chance at something special before it even becomes a chance," Brand counseled sharply.

"You're right, but once you've been kicked in the teeth by a mule, it's hard to want to step behind one again."

"You're the one who's got to work on that. Right now, I'd better go see what I can do to make amends with my wife."

"Maybe it would help if I go apologize first," Dallas volunteered.

"By the look on her face, I don't think she'll want you near her," Brand said solemnly, hoping she would let him near.

Ca&a

Rachael couldn't keep the tears back. By the time she reached their room, throwing herself on the bed, the tears became sobs. She buried her face in the pillow to hold back the sound though it failed to hold back the pain.

It was all a deception because of Brand's guilt over the loss of her innocence. How could she be so stupid to believe? Everyone must think it was some joke, that Brand would marry someone like her. And as soon as they knew about the baby, they'd all know why Brand married her.

She didn't belong here. Pushing up from the bed, she looked around the room, swiping back the tears. She needed to think but not here. Not where Brand was stamped so heavy. Not where they had slept together.

Rachael didn't even think where she was going as she ran down the stairs and out the door. At the garage, she only paused long enough to realize she had no car. Taking the path, she headed for the stables. Boosting the saddle on Sugar Baby's back, she jerked when she heard someone behind her. Glancing back, she was relieved it wasn't Brand as she feared.

"Would you like a hand with that?" John asked from the door.

"No, thanks." She averted her face. "I can manage."

The man paused a moment before he left.

With a sigh, Rachael tightened the cinch. Grabbing the reins she swung into the saddle, giving Sugar a kick. The horse took off, moving into a strong gallop then a run. The ground blurred even more from the tears.

She wanted to go home, to her home. She was foolish to let herself fall in love and believe that Brand could love her. Hadn't she known all along she didn't fit into his world? The only reason she was there was the baby.

Her tears fell harder. Slowing the horse to a walk she leaned forward wrapping her arms around its neck. The baby, what was going to happen to the baby? If she left and Brand took it from her, she'd die, but she couldn't survive here loving Brand and knowing he didn't love her.

She tried to think, but the tears kept coming down. She didn't think where she was going, just letting Sugar take her until the opening in the trees revealed the frame house Brand was working on. It was to be their house. They'd spent several hours over here while he moved the one wall frame and made a few changes for her studio.

He had gotten someone out to do the electrical, the insulation and drywall, which he said was something he didn't want to do anyway. It was beginning to look like a house, but it would never be her home. Tears came again.

With a slight motion, Sugar started back toward the road. At the white board fence, she turned and followed it toward the highway. Tears still trickled down her cheeks, but she was calmer.

Maybe she would still move here. There was no family keeping her in Wyoming. She had no one but the baby that grew in her. She couldn't keep the baby from Brand, and if she lived close enough, she didn't think he would take it from her. And when it was old enough and she had to continue her work, he could help take care of it.

It was a good thing she got the calendar deal. She wouldn't have to work for at least a year after the baby was born. She could see how many pictures she could stockpile now before she started getting large, by then winter would be here. She always cut back her trips then.

She was so lost in thought the crack of a rifle shot didn't quite register in her mind until Sugar sprang forward in a mad charged across the ground. One rein slipped from her hand and flopped dangerously near the horse's hooves.

"Whoa," she cried urgently, trying to use the one rein while clinging to the saddle and dodging tree limbs. Sugar brushed past a tree nearly swiping Rachael from the saddle. She had almost regained her seat on her wild ride when Sugar's hoof clipped a rock and she stumbled.

Already off balance, Rachael felt herself leave the saddle. No way to stop the fall, she hit the ground hard and tumbled. Her hip hit a rock sending a jolt of pain through her until her head struck another rock and things went dark.

Chapter Sixteen

Brand opened the door to their room surprised to find Rachael not there. Dashing to the bathroom, she wasn't in there or the walk-in closet either. Back by the bed he paused fingering the indentation in the pillow that was shifted out of place. It was damp. He bit back a curse.

How could he have been so stupid to blurt out her innocence? Images of her pale, stricken face flashed in his mind. He'd hurt her. "Rachael!" he yelled checking every room on a run. "Rachael!" he called on the stairs.

"What's wrong?" Dallas yelled back, running into the family room.

"Rachael's not upstairs."

They split up without a word, checking the main floor. Martha was in the kitchen as Brand entered.

"Have you seen Rachael?"

"She was out on the patio eating breakfast."

"She's gone. I can't find her."

"Not here," Dallas said entering from the garage.

"She doesn't have a car," Brand answered already heading out. They checked the pool, gazebo and the yard before heading to the stable.

"You think she'd come here?" Dallas asked as he caught up to him again.

"It's possible, she likes to ride and be outdoors. It actually makes sense. John!" he yelled for his foreman. "Have you seen Rachael?"

"Yeah, she rode out of here about twenty ago. She was acting kind of funny. She didn't stop to talk at all. Is anything wrong?"

"Yeah, saddle Torrent for me." Brand ran to get a radio. "Call me if she comes back," he told Dallas.

"Sure. Let me know when you find her."

Brand nodded.

"Listen, I'm sorry. I was just …" Dallas' words died out. "I'm sorry."

"Me, too." Brand grabbed the horse's reins as John led him out. "Which way did she go?" He swung the horse in the direction the foreman indicated and was already moving by the time he had his other foot in the stirrup.

෮෭

Everything was a fog of confusion as Rachael came back to consciousness. Light strained though the leaves. Shifting, she cried out as pain radiated though her hip then ricocheted in her head. For the second time that day, nausea hit her hard and fast, barely giving her time to roll over before she was sick.

With each heave, pain streaked through her abdomen.

"No, the baby," she cried when she could catch her breath. Tears burned her eyes.

Sugar stood nearby. Stumbling to her feet, everything swam around her, and she had to grab hold of the tree trunk to keep from falling. She lowered herself back to the ground.

Her hand trembled as she brushed away the tears running down her cheeks and came back bloody. Feeling her forehead, she found the bump where the blood oozed, but discounted it as another round of pain and nausea hit her.

Wrapping her arms around her stomach, she huddled on the ground hurting too much to move but knew she had to get help. Her next attempt to make it to her feet didn't go any better. Sinking to the ground, she cried, curling on her side as she fought to keep the pain back.

"Brand," she cried his name wanting him more than she ever had. She was unable to stop the tears or fear that she was losing the baby.

The first time she heard Brand calling her name she thought she was hallucinating, but by the time it was called a third time, she fought to answer.

"Brand," her cry was weak and left her mind floating toward unconsciousness.

Brand turned Torrent to what he thought was his name carried on the breeze. He saw Sugar first, but no Rachael. He covered over half the distance before he finally saw her curled on the ground. Panic surged through him.

"Rachael." He hit the ground running before the horse came to a complete stop.

"Brand." Her cry was weak as he dropped beside her. "The baby … please."

"Shh," he reached down to wipe back her hair. His hand came back bloody. He rolled her slightly on her back, filling with terror at the sight of the blood on the side of her head and matted in her hair.

"The baby," she groaned with pain, curling back into a ball as another cramp rippled through her.

He pulled out the radio. "Dallas," he didn't wait for an answer. "Rachael's taken a fall. We have to get her to the hospital fast. We're about a quarter mile past the turn to my place. Fifty feet off the road."

"On my way." The answer came back, but Brand had already tossed the radio to the side.

"Rachael." He tried to get her attention through her tears. "Rachael, you have to tell me where you're hurt," he said running his hands over her now familiar body.

"I fell. I didn't mean to."

"I know."

"Please, don't let me lose the baby."

"I'll get you to the hospital, but you have to calm down and tell me where it hurts."

With a shaky hand, she reached for her head.

He caught it keeping it away from the cut.

"I'm going to be sick again." She rolled to her side. This time it was only dry heaves.

Brand wrapped his arms around her trembling body. "It's going to be all right," he said more to himself.

The truck Dallas was driving skidded to a stop on the road. Brand cradled her up in his arms and stood.

"How is she?" Dallas called getting out of the truck.

"She's moving but in pain. I'm sure she has a concussion. Can you get the horses back? I want to get her to the hospital."

"I'll get someone else to come get them. I better drive so you can hold her."

Brand just nodded. Rachael cried out a couple times as they got her over the fence and into the truck. Brand held her in his arms, while she cried about the baby.

Dallas used the cell phone to call the hospital to warn them they were coming in, and then called the ranch to have the horses brought in.

It took them only eleven minutes to make it to the hospital, a nurse and orderly were waiting with a gurney. Brand barely had time to tell them she was two and a half weeks pregnant before she was taken away from him to the examination room.

He felt Dallas's hand on his shoulder. "Come on, they need some information."

"I can't lose her." The words came out.

"They're doing all they can. Everything will be fine."

"If she loses the baby, I'll lose her." The certainty of it terrified him. He let Dallas direct him through doing the paperwork. His attention remained focused on the closed door that kept him from her. He paced the emergency room for an eternity before he saw the familiar face of Dr. Grayson.

"Didn't expect to see you so soon," the older man greeted him.

"Rachael." His voice broke.

"I know, they called me," he said.

"You've seen her?" Brand pleaded for answers.

"Easy. She's doing fine. She has a concussion and is pretty bruised up, but the uterus seems fine. There's no bleeding. The cramps she was experiencing were probably from the nausea from the concussion, but we want to keep an eye on her for the night. Just for observation. If something happens, it's usually within the first twenty-four hours."

"But she's doing fine? She isn't in danger?"

"No, she isn't in danger. They're about to move her into a room."

"Can I see her now?" he asked anxiously.

"In a minute," the doctor said gently. "Brand, Rachael is very upset still. I don't know what happened, but she needs to stay calm because of the concussion as much as for the baby. You can talk to her, but if she gets upset, you have to go."

"She said she didn't want to see me." He knew it. His heart sank lower.

"Yes, and the next instant she cried for you. She's quite confused. She was afraid she was going to lose the baby. She kept saying you didn't love her."

Brand groaned aloud. "Where is she?"

"Second door on the left, but they've probably already moved her. You'll have to check with the nurse."

"Thanks." Brand headed down the hall. Rachael didn't think he loved her. He turned the thought over in his head. Well, she had another think coming.

Rachael had already been moved, but the nurse directed him to her room. Brand arrived in time to see the nurse leaving. He paused in the doorway. Rachael lay in the only occupied bed in the room. Her eyes were closed. From the faint light above the bed, he could see the glisten of a tear in the corner of her eye.

Silently, he moved to the bed extending his hand. He stopped a fraction from her hair. "Oh, my little love, what am I going to do with you?" He dropped to the chair pushing his fingers into his hair.

"Brand."

He lifted his head to find her looking at him. "How are you feeling?" He sat forward.

"The doctor said everything's okay, but I have a concussion."

"I know, he told me. You're supposed to stay still."

"He said the baby was fine, but they want to keep me overnight."

"Yes, sweetheart, I'm so sorry. The way it sounded, I didn't mean to blurt your innocence out like that. I was just mad that Dallas was getting on you, and I just wanted him to shut up. It came out sounding all wrong."

"I … I …" Tears welled up in her eyes and flowed over.

"Oh, sweetheart, don't cry. If I upset you, they'll kick me out and I couldn't bear to leave you now. It scared the daylights out of me when I found you." He couldn't resist the need to wipe away the tears.

"I'm sorry, I didn't mean to fall. I wasn't trying to hurt the baby."

"I know. I never thought you were." Brand tried to assure her.

"I thought that you didn't want me. That you really were just guilty because of what happened." She couldn't stop the sob from slipping through.

"No, I promise. Please, believe me, I want you. I want the baby, but baby or not, I would want you still. You've come to mean everything to me. I can't lose you."

"It really was an accident. I wasn't paying attention, so when the shot sounded and Sugar took off, I wasn't ready. She stumbled. Is she all right?"

"I'm sure she's fine. Don't worry. John will take care of her."

"She stumbled," Rachael repeated. It wasn't hard to see her strength fading.

"John will look her over. Don't worry about her. You just worry about getting some rest. I'll be right here."

∞

Rachael closed her eyes and felt Brand's hand slide over hers, interlocking their fingers. She was glad he was there. She felt better from the time she heard him call her his 'little love'. She'd felt his hand hovering over her, and she knew it wasn't a lie. Brand loved her. It was there in his touch.

"I love you," she whispered sleepily.

"I love you, too."

His lips brushed her temple.

Brand was sitting by the bed watching Rachael sleep when Dallas entered the room. "How is she?" he asked.

"Fine, she's sleeping peacefully."

"Did you get to talk to her?"

"Yeah, she was a little out of it, but I think we're okay. I came so close to losing her today. I never want to go through that again." He didn't take his eyes from the bed.

"I'm sorry," Dallas apologized again.

"I should have explained things better. I was going to, but you took off and I didn't get a chance."

"Do you think she'll forgive me? I was pretty awful to her." His voice was full of guilt.

"Probably. She has a very forgiving nature. Sometimes it really blows me away how loving and innocent she is to have survived in this world." He looked up a moment then back to his sleeping wife.

"Well, I'd say she picked herself a good protector."

"I didn't do so hot today."

"I think she'd probably disagree. Besides, you're still learning."

"She seems to get into more trouble than anyone I have ever known."

Dallas laughed at his brother's woes. "I better go before she wakes up."

"It'll probably be better to wait until tomorrow to see you."

"Good idea. What's your plan?"

"I'm going to stay here tonight. I don't want to leave her. Can you drop a car off for me?"

"No problem, anything else?"

"The only thing I want is for her to be all right."

Dallas nodded and left. About ten minutes later the nurse came in. "Oh," she jumped. "Who are you?"

Brand stood extending his hand. "Brand Morgan, I'm Rachael's husband."

"I thought the other guy was?"

"No, that's my brother."

She moved to the bed with a nod. "If you'll excuse me, I have to get vitals and wake your wife."

"Sure."

"Mrs. Morgan I need you to wake up."

Rachael's eyes opened. "Hmmm."

"Can you tell me your full name?"

"Rachael Ann Jacobs Morgan."

"What's your husband's name?"

"Brand." She gave his name in a dreamy tone that Brand loved. He wanted to take her into his arms more than he ever had. Then he had to almost laugh when she was asked, "What day is it?" and answered. "I'm not sure. I lost track." His humor didn't last long when she gasped. "Oh, I'm going to be sick."

When Rachael sat back with a moan, her body shook again.

"It's all right," the nurse assured her while she took care of the pan they used. "The nausea is from your concussion. Since the choice was not to give you something because you're pregnant. It should pass soon. I'll be bringing you something to eat and that might help."

She left and Brand retook his spot beside the bed, brushing back her hair.

"I feel so sick and my head hurts." Tears ran down her cheeks.

"I'm sorry. I wish I could do something to make you feel better."

"I wish you could hold me." She wiped back a tear.

"I think we can manage that." Brand walked around the bed, lowered the side rail and climbed on. "Easy." He shifted her slightly so she lay back against him, her head pillowed against his shoulder.

She wrapped her hands around his biceps and cuddled back.

"Better?" he asked, stroking her with his free hand.

"Much. What time is it?"

He lifted his wrist to see his watch. "Ten to four."

"It seems later."

"Blinds are pulled to keep out the light. Why don't you see if you can get some more rest before your dinner comes?"

She nodded in a snuggling action.

Night progressed much the same way. Brand ate more of her dinner then she did as her stomach was still too unsettled for her to handle it. The nurse didn't say anything about the position they spent the night. Just came in to wake her and do vitals.

She was still cuddled, asleep against him when Dr. Grayson came in the next morning.

"It looks like you got things worked out," he commented to Brand.

"Yes."

"How's she doing?"

"She had a rough night between the nurse waking her and being sick several times."

"I'm afraid that was to be expected, but there were no signs of cramping, which is good. They'll release her about noon. You can take her home and let her get as much sleep as possible," he instructed. "They put four stitches in her head, so I'll need to see her in a week to take them out. Keep an eye on her for a couple days, that shouldn't be too difficult." He smiled.

Brand smiled back, nodded, and Rachael stretched in his arms. A small whimper escaped her bringing open her eyes.

"Good morning," Dr. Grayson greeted her. "I stopped to see how you're feeling and sign a release form for you."

"I can go home?"

"About noon. I gave Brand instructions, so listen to him. You're supposed to stay down for a couple days, until your headaches go away. You can take something for it now. There are no signs of complications. If you have any signs of pain, I want to know immediately and no more riding horses. You don't want to risk another fall."

"Believe me, it won't happen again. I'll stay off the horses," she promised. "But it wouldn't have happened if the shot hadn't spooked Sugar Baby."

"Shot?" Dr. Grayson asked, looking at Brand who shrugged. When she mentioned it before, he thought it was her mind playing tricks.

"Yes. It startled me, it was so close. I dropped the reins. I was trying to get them when Sugar stumbled."

"What do you mean close?" This time it was Brand that asked the question.

"It almost hit me. I would almost think someone was shooting at me, but I know that's ridiculous, but it did startle Sugar."

"You think someone shot at you?" Brand pressed.

"No, that's crazy. Why would anyone?" Even though her denial was strong, Brand felt her hand tighten on his arm.

He waited until the doctor left before he addressed her on the shot again. He shifted her so he could look down at her. "You really are scared."

Her eyes dropped. "I know I'm just being paranoid after what happened before, but the shot wasn't my imagination. I know it wasn't."

"I didn't say it was, but who would want to hurt you here?"

"I don't know." A tear still lingering near the surface welled to escaping.

"It wasn't Dallas, I promise. When I found you missing, he helped me search the house. He's really feeling guilty about what happened. If you lost the baby, he never would have forgiven himself and if anything would have happened to you … I never want to feel like that again. I love you."

"Then you better take good care of me." With a gentle pull from her hand, he came down to kiss her.

He was still kissing her when the nurse came in. "I thought I wasn't going to have any trouble with you."

"You're not." Brand slid off the bed, looking decidedly embarrassed. "I'm going down the hall a minute."

"Honey, you're in for trouble with that one." The nurse chuckled. "But boy is that my brand of trouble."

At the words, a smile crested Rachael's lips. "No, that's my Brand of trouble," she said firmly getting a full blood laughed from the nurse.

ALYSIA S. KNIGHT

Chapter Seventeen

Brand wasn't sure what he thought of the possibility of someone taking a shot at Rachael until he got back to the ranch and talked to John. Rachael was so concerned about Sugar Baby that as soon as he got her settled in bed, he went to check on the horse. John told him she was fine except for a scrape. When Brand looked at the scrape, he felt a shiver race through him as he studied the half inch score that creased the horse's rump.

After reassuring Rachael that Sugar was all right he waited until she fell asleep before he made a call to the Las Vegas Police Department. Neither Sullivan nor Rawlins were in. The officer he talked to checked and confirmed that Chantell was still in custody, which really didn't ease his worry.

They were at the breakfast table the next morning when the phone rang and Dallas answered it. "Brand, it's for you, a Detective Sullivan."

The little gasp from Rachael caught his attention. "It's all right. I called him." He reached for her hand giving it a squeeze before he left the table.

When he returned, he found Dallas trying to keep her entertained. At least one good thing had come from what happened. Dallas had apologized, Rachael had forgiven him, and they were now becoming friends.

"Brand?" Rachael looked to him.

"Chantell is still in custody undergoing psychiatric evaluation. Sullivan's not sure if they'll find her fit to stand

180

trial. She pretty much flipped out. Now don't look like that, it's not your fault," Brand insisted.

"Sullivan said it looks like her problem goes way back to her childhood. He also said the police in her home town are taking another look into her father's death. It was supposed to have been a hiking accident, now they're not sure."

"Heavens," Emily Morgan exclaimed. "What a disturbed woman."

"She is, but they're trying to help her," Brand commented back. "I'm just glad she can't get near Rachael."

"But you still believe I heard a shot?"

"Yes, but I'm hoping it was an accident or that you were at the wrong place at the wrong time." Brand took her hand rubbing his thumb over her knuckles.

"You think someone might have been looking for the mountain lion?" Dallas asked.

"What mountain lion?" Rachael honed in on that.

"A cougar appeared while Brand was gone." Dallas continued, "The next ranch over lost a couple calves. It was spotted on our ranch yesterday morning. So far we haven't lost anything, but a lot of men are carrying rifles just in case. It's possible someone thought they were firing at the cougar, but they'd have to be pretty jumpy to mistake a rider on horseback for one."

"If I find out that's what happened, they'll be wearing that rifle for a necklace." There was fire in Brand's eyes as he thought of what could have happened to her. He wanted to send Rachael right back to their bed.

"Are you going to track him?" Rachael turned to Brand, her thoughts obviously still on the cougar.

"Not yet, I'm hoping it will just move on, but if not, we'll have to trap him."

"Can we try to find him? I'd like to get some shots."

"No!" Brand said firmly, heaven save him.

"But they're so hard to find and if we can find him. Please Brand."

"You're supposed to be resting."

"I have been."

"Rachael, you have a concussion." He stood moving back a couple steps as if some distance would give him strength against her.

"But," she looked pleadingly and he knew space wasn't helping. She had his number, but this time he refused to give in.

"I'll tell you what. Odds are he'll move on, but if it stays around and we have to go after it." He held up his hand to stop her comment. "And if you have been staying down resting, we'll talk about taking you with us, as long as I'm sure you'll be safe. And, that is if the Fish and Game will allow it. It will be their show, so their call."

"That's a lot of ifs." She frowned, obviously not happy.

"That's how it's going to be." He crossed his arms over his chest to show her he meant every word.

"You're getting pretty domineering." She scowled and crossed her own arms in front of her, not bothering to hide her displeasure.

"I'm not going to risk you getting hurt."

Her frown remained, but she shrugged. "All right, I'll stay down and behave if you promise."

"I promise."

Three days later he wished he could take the promise back when the cat went after another calf before disappearing onto his property. With no choice, Brand contacted the Fish and Game and organized the hunt with them and the guys from the other ranch for the next morning.

He wished he could think of a way not to tell Rachael, but he knew he couldn't keep it from her. "You know the chances of you seeing the cat aren't good? Dr. Grayson said no horses, and I'm not going to risk you on a jumpy horse because there's a mountain lion around."

"I understand the odds, and I won't risk a horse either." She met him straight on. "But I still want to go."

He gave in with a huff, pushing his fingers back through his hair. "Fine, we'll be in the Jeep."

"That's fine."

He knew he was getting himself in trouble. "You're going?"

"Did you really think that would discourage me?"

"No, but I hoped," he grumped.

Rachael smiled and stepped forward, sliding her arms around his neck. "Poor baby," she cooed. Brushing her lips across his while he tried to ignore her.

"I'm in trouble."

"You got it." She found his lips for a light kiss.

"Why'd you have to learn to flirt?" He groaned and she laughed, getting into the effort to make him feel better.

 CRED

It was forty minutes before sunrise when Brand picked up Rachael's camera bag and cooler, and they headed to the open yard by the stables where they would meet the others.

John and another of their men, Milt, were already there saddling up horses. A couple minutes later, Dallas joined them as two trucks with horse trailers pulled up.

"Brent." Brand greeted as the man stepped out. "Mornin'."

Rachael was surprised when Brenda slid from the truck.

"Good morning," the woman said pushing her hands into the pockets of her already tight jeans. She went right to Brand's side. "I didn't expect to see you." She glanced to Rachael.

Brand beat her to the answer. "Rachael's hoping to get some pictures of the cougar."

"Oh, I just thought she would be in bed still. I heard about the accident." Her voice dripped with a sympathy Rachael didn't like.

"Rachael and I will be in the Jeep."

"Oh, that's too bad." Brenda laid her hand on Brand's sleeve. "You can ride with me if you need a partner. I know how you love to ride. It really is too bad you're stuck with a wife who can't keep up with you."

"Rachael's an excellent rider. She's just grounded for a while, and I don't mind being in the Jeep, especially with my partner." He stepped closer to Rachael, sliding his arms around her.

Erik Young from the Fish and Game took that moment to approach them. "All right everyone has a radio and each team has a tranquilizer gun and a rifle. Remember we want to tranquilize the animal if possible, but we don't want anyone hurt."

"All set, Erik. I don't think you've had the opportunity to meet my wife, Rachael. Rachael, this is Erik Young." They shook hands. "Rachael and I will head to the ridge while you guys work your way up the gullies. Be careful."

An hour and a half later, Brand was once again debating the wisdom of letting Rachael come along. The road was rough, bouncing her all over the place.

"Are you okay?" he asked glancing her way.

"I'm fine for the fourth time in ten minutes. No headache, no morning sickness, nothing to worry about."

"Right."

"Brand, I'm all right. I'm not going to do anything to endanger myself or the baby. I have learned my lesson. Please relax and enjoy the scenery. I am. It's beautiful here. Look at the sun coming off the cliffs.

"Would you like to stop and take a picture of them?"

"That's not necessary. You're driving slower than a hundred and two year old grandmother on her way to church."

"It's rough and I'm not that bad," he grumbled.

"Yes, you are and I love you for it." She slid her hand over his on the gearshift.

"Brand," Dallas's voice came over the radio.

"Here," Brand answered back.

"We're in Hopkins gulch. Erik thought he saw a movement coming up the lower edge of the cliffs above us. We have tracks all over here like it's been coming and going this way."

"Figures. Okay. We're just about at the big group of boulders on the rise. We'll stop where we can scan the whole area and the mouth of the gulch."

He shifted back into gear, climbing the rise before he stopped again. "That's Hopkins gulch." He pointed about three hundred yards to the north. "Dallas and Erik should be about a quarter mile down it still. Brent and Brenda should be coming up the draw on the other side of them and their other two men on the one over there. John and Milt are just south of us." This road goes all the way across then splits and cuts up the hill again or down toward the Bar-B."

He picked up the binoculars and started scanning the top of the gulch, while Rachael used her camera.

"I have another set of binoculars," he said.

"No thanks, I prefer this, its lens is just as powerful as a spotting scope."

"I still can't believe you brought all this equipment with you on your trip."

"Never leave home without them. Actually, I was planning to use my extra day to go out to the desert to shoot."

"You didn't get your chance to do that." He felt a twinge of regret for her.

"It's okay. This makes up for it," she assured him.

"Just this?"

"Yeah, there's nothing in my life that equals marrying you."

"I hope that's meant in a good way."

"The best." She blushed and looked away.

"I guess now isn't the best time to make out in a car." He leaned over to her. "But you sure make it tempting."

She looked back over in surprise.

"I'll have to settle for a quick kiss." He came forward and was gone in just enough time to leave her lips tingling and her eyes wide as a startled deer. "You're supposed to be looking out there instead of at me," he said smugly.

"Right." She turned her attention back through the camera, but the smile remained on her lips.

After a couple minutes the radio again broke the silence. "Have you seen anything yet?" The other groups ran through their negative answers.

"Nothing's come out of the gully so far," Brand said when it was his turn. "How far are you from the top?"

"About an eighth of a mile, we're still seeing plenty of tracks."

"Brand," Rachael's whispered exclamation took his attention from the radio as he heard her camera snap off three shots.

"Do you see him?"

"Not him. Look up there, the boulders then just to the right of them. Do you see?" Her voice remained as a whisper.

"I don't see."

"Keep watching."

"We're supposed to be watching for mountain lions."

"You are. Cubs, three of them I think," she said swing her legs from the Jeep.

"Where are you going?"

"I want to get closer."

"No way, this changes the whole thing. We don't have an out of location or a sick animal. We've a mother feeding and protecting her young." He could feel the hairs on his neck raise.

"I understand all that. That's why she's coming down to the ranches, easier and more constant supply of food," Rachael said.

"Yeah, but I want to see what Erik wants to do about this, if he wants to try to move the family or not. So stay here."

"I'm just going to the next rise for a better look," she said gently.

"No."

"It's only fifty feet, and I'll be in your view the whole time."

"Rachael." He tried to argue.

"Brand, I promise, I won't take chances. I have my own baby to protect."

"No more than fifty feet." He gave in against his wishes.

"I promise." She crossed her heart before carefully making her way up the slope to the next set of boulders.

Brand broke out in a sweat as he picked up the binoculars and the radio. "Dallas."

"Yeah, come back."

"Is Erik close?"

"Right here."

"Good. Things have changed. It looks like our mountain lion is a mama. Rachael just spotted cubs. Three, she thinks. I'm still trying to locate them. There, I got two in sight, about half way between the top of the gulch and our location. They're little, the den must be just right there in the rocks. They're not big enough to be away from it. There's number three, a feisty little guy."

He watched the cub attack his sibling from above. He wondered if Rachael was watching their antics. Shifting his attention her way, she had kept her word not going farther than fifty feet. She was plastered to the rock. Her total attention focused on the cubs. He saw her switch cameras then after a minute jerk back. Glancing his way to see if he was watching, she motioned to the side.

It only took him a second to spot the big cat even though she blended in perfectly with her terrain.

"We've got the female in sight. She just came out of the gulch not really concerned about your presence yet. She's a big thing," he said in the radio. Glancing back to Rachael, she was switching cameras again. Brand whispered a curse. She was a lot closer to the animal than he liked. Little fool, she didn't even have a gun on her.

"Erik, what are we going to do, try moving her or not?"

"We've got to move her." The Fish and Game officer's voice came through the radio. "She's too close to people. Someone will end up shooting her, and we'll lose the cubs to scavengers. If they do survive, we'll have more trouble to contend with in the future."

"All right, I'm going to move up a little closer to Rachael."

"Where's Rachael?" Dallas asked.

"Taking pictures of course," he snarled then added. "She's at a safe distance."

"Poor guy," he heard his brother say before he continued. "Let us get a little farther up the gulch, and then when you get an open shot with the tranquilizer, take it. Erik said don't hit the cubs, these darts are too powerful. We'll catch them by hand."

"I'll have to get closer for a good shot."

"Okay, give us ten minutes to get into position, then just use vibrate. We'll buzz you twice when we see her. Give us three when you're set to fire."

Brand clipped the radio to his belt and took the dart gun, checking its load then he made his way to Rachael.

"Can you believe this?" she whispered as he approached.

"Yeah." From there he could see the cubs plainly without the binoculars.

They watched the cubs greet and romp on their mother. The big animal, whose paws were several times the size of the cub's heads, and teeth that could rip them apart, was incredibly gentle in her play.

Beside Brand, Rachael's camera whirled not making any more noise than a grasshopper in flight. He knew she was getting the kitten after its mother's tail and the other two attacking at her head. Glancing at his watch it was almost time to move forward.

"I have to move into position," he whispered in her ear.

"Just a minute, let me change lens."

"You're staying here." The look she gave him let him know he'd already lost that argument. "So much for the obey part," he whispered resigned.

"I'm sorry, but this is what I do," Rachael said looking up from her camera. "If it makes it easier, I have the love and honor down."

"Two out of three's not bad, I guess." This time it was said playfully.

"I'll work on the other. Let's go." Crouching, she slipped from behind the boulder leaving him to follow.

With a shrug, he followed, admiring the way she moved. It was with the same stealth she had the morning by the lake. Moving with cover, she paused, he realized to check the direction of the slight breeze that had come up. She motioned that it was coming off the mountain, which was good for them.

Brand nodded, directing her toward the location he wanted to head. Rachael nodded back then stepped aside for him to pass her and lead the way. From where he first planned, he couldn't get a good view of the cats so he moved on with Rachael right behind him, which put them a lot closer to the cougars than he intended. He could tell

Rachael didn't mind. Her attention focused with the camera, her face a light with expectation and awe.

She was so beautiful he had to force his attention away. He couldn't concentrate on her now. On his belt, he felt the radio vibrate twice letting him know Dallas and Erik were in position so they could see the cats. He scanned the area but couldn't see them, but he could see Brenda across the way with the tranquilizer gun already at her shoulder.

Rachael kept shooting as he pressed the radio three times in return then raised his gun. His view was perfect. He moved the safety off as he fingered the trigger. He was about to fire when Rachael jerked beside him. Her camera clattered to the ground. She shot up, slipping off the side of the boulder before falling to the ground.

Brand's wasn't the only attention that shifted to Rachael. The cougar reacted, springing to her feet. She covered the first twelve feet in a single bound. Brand tried to get a shot off, but his aim was behind the animal as it leapt. The aggravated cougar covered the space in amazing speed. Brand had no time to reach for another dart. Leaping from the boulder, he hit the animal just before it pounced on Rachael.

He and the animal both tumbled to the ground. Now he had the cat's attention, he wasn't sure what to do with it. The cat, only four feet from him, made the decision for him. Pushing off the ground, it came for him. The impact sent them both to the ground again, but this time the cat came down on top of him with all the advantages. In self-defense, Brand grabbed the neck trying to keep the jaws and vicious teeth back.

Rachael's scream blended with the cat's, but he was too busy to notice. Expecting at any minute to feel the claws tear though his denim jacket into his skin. The powerful cat pressed closer. Brand could smell and feel the breath on his face. He was sure he was going to feel the sharp teeth when there was a hiss from the tranquilizer gun.

The cougar jerked then second later it swayed and fell on him, still, but breathing.

"Brand." Rachael dropped the gun then was by him, pushing the unconscious animal away. "Where are you hurt?" She clawed at him, searching for cuts and scrapes.

"I'm all right," he insisted, but her hands kept up their feverish search until she was satisfied, then she threw her arms around his neck, hugging him to her. The camera that hung around her neck jabbed him in the chest, he didn't complain feeling her tears.

"What happened?" Dallas and Erik charged up. "Are you hurt?"

"No, no I'm okay."

"Good. What happened?" Dallas repeated.

Rachael had been trying to compose herself. She sat back, wiping away her tears.

"Rachael slipped and dropped her camera. It startled the cougar and it attacked."

Dallas's curse startled her. "She shouldn't have been this close. You could've been killed."

That brought her out of her stupor. "It wasn't my fault. I was shot at and stumbled back. What would you have done?"

"Shot at," Erik said. He and Dallas exchanged looks both had the same disbelieving look.

"There wasn't a shot," Dallas said.

"There was too." Rachael looked to Brand for confirmation.

He just looked back and shook his head. "There wasn't a shot."

ॐ

Rachael felt the tears start to well up again. His eyes said he didn't believe her. She wondered if he believed her the last time or if he'd just been trying to pacify her like his next words.

"It's all right, no harm done. You even saved my hide, shooting the cougar. She's down for a nice long nap."

"But I wouldn't have had to if I didn't goof up," Rachael added what she knew they were thinking. "Well, I didn't goof up. I didn't just slip. I know what I'm doing out here and have as much or more experience stalking animals as any of you. I say I was shot at and I was. If it hadn't hit my camera, it would have hit—" She stopped in midsentence.

"My camera!" she cried scrambling over the rocks to retrieve it. Even before she picked it up, she knew it was broken. Groaning, tears rose again. They didn't stop when she saw the object that was lodged in between the camera and the strap ring.

"Is it broken?" Brand asked from behind her where they were checking out the cat.

"The lens is. I'll have to check out the camera later. Here you might want it though." She turned back and handed it to him. Aware he looked as confused as the other men, she added. "I'd be careful how you handle it though. You might end up taking that long nap along with our mama." She shifted her gaze to him.

"What?" He looked down and for the first time Rachael heard him swear out loud.

Rachael turned away.

"Rachael," he called her, but she wasn't in any mood to listen. Her throat constricted. She hurt too much inside. "I'm going to see if I can find the cubs." She kept her back to him, but before she could walk off, Brenda and her father rode up.

"Is everyone okay?" the woman asked hurriedly as she looked at the camera in Brand's hand. "I'm so sorry. I slipped and hit the trigger. I can't believe it came that close to you. Your camera's broke," she continued. "I'll buy you a new one."

"Don't worry about it. I'll take care of it," Brand spoke up.

Rachael didn't acknowledge either. "If you'll excuse me, I want to get some shots of the cubs." She walked away with her spare camera, her heart beating painfully in her chest. She still felt like crying, but she wouldn't.

Climbing over the rocks, she worked her way to where she'd seen the cubs. It took a minute before she finally located them hidden in the rocks. She switched lenses and added a flash to her remaining camera before shooting a dozen pictures all the while talking in a soothing voice to the wide-eyed cubs.

"Rachael." She heard Brand say her name as he came up behind her.

"Please stay back. They're frightened enough as it is." She continued to take pictures, moving slightly for a different angle. "There's a fourth one that must have been in here sleeping." She removed the flash and changed the setting before bring the camera back to her eyes.

"John and Milt are bringing up the cage from the Jeep. Rachael, will you look at me."

Tears blurred her focus but she blinked them away, taking another shot. "I want to get as many shots as I can before we have to move them." She knew he stood behind her but refused to acknowledge him further.

"Rachael."

Her hand froze in motion before continuing.

"I'm sorry." The words were thick with sincerity. He waited for her to answer.

"Me too," she finally said so soft she wasn't sure he heard it before she refocused it on one of the kittens who decided he was more interested in one of the others ears than her. Behind, she heard Brand move away.

Chapter Eighteen

Erik was still checking the cougar out when Brand made it back to them. Dallas looked up from where he was assisting. "She all right?"

"No, she has a jerk for a husband."

"Come on, it isn't that bad," Dallas returned.

"No. I just said I thought she was lying. I criticized her abilities and broke her camera, which are like her babies."

"You didn't break her camera," Dallas pointed out.

"Thanks. How about this? She's worried about me and did I hold her and calm her, no."

"Oh, Brand." Brenda spoke, coming over to lay her hand on his arm, sidling up close, as she seemed to being doing a lot. "You're being too hard on yourself. Some women are just overly sensitive and there is no pleasing them. It's just too bad you didn't know it before you married her."

He looked back toward Rachael to find she was finally looking at him. When her gaze sharpened on the other woman's hand on his arm before turning away, he felt an even stronger sense of dread.

Shaking off Brenda's hand he moved away. "I'll go help them with the cage."

With the cougar loaded, they began the process of catching the cubs. They came out little balls of spitting and swatting fur, but once they were placed with their mother, they calmed, though they really didn't like the Jeep ride.

Brand noticed Rachael didn't seem any more pleased with it. She gripped the roll bar, her attention focused on the cats. Several times he tried to ask her questions, but they were returned with short or one-word answers.

Because of care for the animals, they had to keep their speed slow so they got back to the ranch just after the riders. It took some effort to transfer the cage to the Fish and Game truck.

Rachael stayed around taking more pictures which she promised to give Erik a set for their records to show the capture and move of the cougar. When the man said good-bye and left, she returned to the Jeep to get her camera bag. She noticed Brand had put the broken camera in the bag with the dart removed.

"Sorry about that." Brenda came up beside her. "As I said, I'll buy you a new one if it will make you feel better."

"There's no need, Brand said he would take care of it." Rachael tried to sound pleasant.

"Brand's so great about taking care of everything. He always has looked out for me."

Rachael knew the woman was being catty and decided not to stick around and let her get to her. "Yes, well, if you'll excuse me. I want to check over my camera."

"What's your problem?" the woman said loudly when she turned away. "It's not like I shot at you on purpose."

"Brenda." Her father came over.

"No, she thinks I shot at her. You'd think I was trying to kill her or something. Well even if it hit her, all it would have done was put her to sleep and Erik had the antidote. Maybe you think I did it so the cougar would attack you, like I knew what it would do. You think I would have endangered Brand's life that way. He could've been hurt trying to save you." The woman was almost was shrieking.

"Brenda!" her father said firmly. "I'm sure Rachael didn't think any such thing."

Brand came up beside them and was surprised when Brenda turned to plaster herself to him.

Watching the scene, Rachael shook her head. "I hadn't." Rachael left it like that. "Excuse me." She walked toward the house keeping her stride smooth until she passed the cover of the trees, then she broke into a run.

Brand watched Rachael go over Brenda's head. The feel of the woman against him left him cold. The sight of Rachael walking away gave him another chill. Again, he knew he wasn't consoling the woman he should be. Again, Rachael was the loser, and he felt he was too.

"Brent." He looked to Brenda's father. "I'm sure Rachael didn't mean to make it sound like an accusation or anything."

"I'm sure the woman's just upset. To think, you and Brenda have been so close forever. She's just jealous of the relationship you two have. It's understandable. Any woman would have problems with it. Considering everyone always figured you and Brenda would get married."

Another chill passed through him. "There's never been anything between Brenda and me," he tried to say it plainly.

"Brenda's always told me everything about your relationship. That's why it was such a shock you getting caught in such a situation, but I'm sure you'll work it out."

"Brent." He started to ask what the man was talking about, but Brenda cut him off, pulling away.

"Daddy, I'd like to go home now." She took her father's arm leading him away.

"That was a nice scene." Dallas came up.

"Oh yeah."

"Feel like you got caught in the middle."

"I feel like Rachael got cut out."

"Come on, you don't really think she thinks that Brenda shot at her on purpose. I mean that's ridiculous."

"Yeah, well, she also noticed the other rifle on Brenda's horse," he pointed out. Not sure what he was going to believe at the moment.

"You don't think."

"No, of course not. I mean why would she? But someone did shoot at Rachael. I found the mark on Sugar Baby." He thought out loud.

"But that doesn't mean it was Brenda. It's as she said, what would have happened if the dart hit her? Put her to sleep. Erik had the antidote. It's not like it would've hurt her." Dallas tried to reason.

"What about the baby. It could've been harmed." Brand was still not ready to give up his fear.

"Does Brenda know Rachael's pregnant?"

"No. No one but you, mom and Candy," Brand said slowly. "Listen, I'd like to get back to the house." He needed to see Rachael to relieve the anxiety he was feeling.

"Good luck."

"Maybe you should wish me common sense. That seems to be what I'm lacking lately." He tried to make light of it.

"No, just your woman skills, and I'm afraid I've been out of the circle too long to be much help there."

"You're thinking about rejoining?"

"I don't know. Maybe if someone like what you found comes my way." His grin became a full smile.

"Then I'll say good luck. Can you help finish up here?"

"Sure."

ᏨᏮ

Rachael was in their room. She was tense when he came up and put his arms around her. "How's your camera?"

"It looks okay. I'll have to run a set through it to know for sure."

"What are you doing now?"

"Deciding what I need to take with me tomorrow." She stepped out of his hold.

"All you'll need is your overnight bag. You'll have all your clothes there already." He had a sinking feeling her thoughts weren't along those lines. Her next words confirmed it.

"I was thinking of maybe taking my new pants so I could get some wear out of them while they still fit." She moved across the room from him.

"How come I get the feeling you won't be back?" He followed her.

"I'll be back. I promise. I've just decided to take some more time. Do some developing, maybe some mounting and painting. Take time to think."

"Of us?"

She nodded.

"And how long do you think this will take?" he asked.

"I don't know. I want to move before I get very big," she said simply.

"You're talking of months. Rachael, you're talking about not coming back to me at all."

"I said I'd come back."

"But it won't be to live with me," he stated what was becoming obvious.

"Listen, Brand, don't worry about it. I won't ever keep you from the baby," she assured him.

"I'm worried about being kept from you," he shot back.

"Come on, you didn't want me in the first place. You were stuck with me, out of guilt. I don't fit into your life."

"Wrong," he cut her off. "You fit perfectly and I wanted you from the first moment I saw you. After that first hour I knew you were the one for me," he pressed, coming up behind her, placing a hand on her shoulder.

"Don't say things like that." Her voice was an agonized cry. "I'm trying to be reasonable here." She took a deep breath. "Look, there's nothing keeping me in Wyoming. So I'll move here. Get a place close. I just, well, I'd like to stay married until after the baby's born. I think it's important."

"But you won't be living with me through your pregnancy," he said pointedly.

"I think you'd just as soon miss that, big, fat, and moody part, but if you want to be there when the baby's born." She let it hang but he didn't.

"No," he said it so harshly that she turned in surprise. Unshed tears hung ready to fall.

"I want to be there every minute, night and day. The thin and the huge and I will live with the moody."

"Please Brand, be reasonable."

"I am being reasonable. You're the one that's running away to hide," he accused.

"I'm not." She turned back away.

"Aren't you? What did you just do, turn away from me."

"I'm not hiding. I'm trying to keep from crying," she said harshly.

"Why would you cry?" he said more softly.

Suddenly her head tilted back as she looked to the ceiling and a loud sob escaped her. "Because I'm being torn up inside and it's killing me." She crumbled into tears this time back into his arms. "No." She tried to struggle free.

"Yes," he said firmly. "I'm not letting you go." He tightened his hold. "If you're going to Wyoming, I'm going too."

"No."

"Yes, I'm not letting you leave me."

"You can wait until I call you," she tried.

"No, I'll go with you tomorrow."

"What about bringing the trailer?"

"I'll rent one or have a moving van come in," he said simply. "It doesn't matter as long as I stay with you. If you want to stay in Wyoming, then I'll stay there with you."

"You can't do that."

"I can if that's what it takes to be with you. I'm so sorry about what happened. If I could go back and do it different, I would. I should've believed you about the dart. It was just so incredulous. I promise, sweetheart. I'll never doubt you again and I don't doubt your abilities. It just scared me to have you so close to danger. I didn't handle it very well. I guess that's my only excuse. I love you."

When he tried to kiss her this time, she didn't resist and after a second she opened to him, letting it grow. When he lifted her into his arms, she wrapped her arms around his neck.

Chapter Nineteen

Brand just closed his bag when the phone rang. He picked it up, watching as Rachael came out of the bathroom wearing his shirt. When she saw him, she gave him a shy smile before disappearing into the closet. Life was good again.

"Yeah," he remembered what he was doing and said into the phone. He listened for a minute. "I'll get someone out there. Thanks." He disconnected then dialed John's number. When no one answered, he tried the stables getting the same response. He glanced at his watch. They had an hour before they had to leave to catch their flight.

"Rachael."

"Yes." She stepped from the closet.

"That was the sheriff's office. Someone called to say one my stallions is out. I can't get anyone down at the stables so I'm going to have to go get it. I should be back long before we have to leave."

"All right, I'll be ready when you get back."

Brand was only gone about five minutes when the doorbell rang. Knowing she was the only one left in the house, Rachael hurried to get it.

"Brenda," she exclaimed finding the woman there.

"Hi, I ran into Brand on the road, and he asked me to give you a ride to the airport," she said in a cheerful tone that was utterly false.

"Oh." Rachael was taken back.

"Come on, we can leave now."

"Actually, I think I'll wait for Brand." She tried to hide a shiver of unease, moving to close the door. "There's plenty of time still."

"Brand said he didn't think he'd make it back. It's going to take him longer to find the horse. I told him I was going that way and could take you, but I have a meeting so I need to leave now." The woman stepped forward.

"But Brand's planning on going with me. I better call the airport and change to a later flight." Rachael stepped back beginning to feel afraid.

"Don't worry. He'll take care of it later. He said he would be a couple of days."

"Oh well, you don't have to bother to take me then I'll just take one of the spare vehicles and leave it in the airport parking."

"No, Brand doesn't want you to do that," the woman insisted.

Rachael's fear rose to terror. "I'm afraid I'll have to insist on driving myself. Thank for the offer." Rachael tried again to close the door on the woman.

"And I'm afraid that I will have to insist you come with me." Brenda pushed back on the door. Her right hand came from behind her holding a handgun that Rachael didn't doubt was loaded.

"What are you doing?" Rachael stepped back but tried to remain calm.

Brenda followed her in. "I'm getting rid of Brand's mistake. He would do this for me. How can I do less for him? It's not right for him to be trapped, tied to you when you're not right for him."

"And I suppose you are?" Rachael asked.

"Of course, it's always been us. Together since we were children in school. I supported him, and he was always there for me. My guardian." The gleam in the woman's eyes was totally eerie.

"So it must've really gotten to you when he risked his life to save me." Rachael wasn't sure what to say just that she needed to keep her talking so she could think.

"It was a natural instinct for him, but once you're out of his life, you'll slip from his mind and then I will be there just like it always was to be."

"You really can't believe it'll be that easy to get Brand." Rachael knew it was probably foolish to challenge her, but couldn't stop herself.

"Of course it will. I've been waiting a long time. My mistake was not realizing he was ready. All the other men were just while waiting. That's why I could never get serious or love any of them. They weren't Brand."

"So you would use them."

"They got what they wanted. They were just foolish if they thought they'd get the Bar-B. It was destined only to be Brand."

"B, Brent, Brenda, Brand." Rachael felt sick.

"Yes, you can see. It has to be him. He was never for you. You're his mistake. Since Brand won't get rid of you, I will, and then he can come to me."

Because of what had happened in Vegas, Rachael knew what she was facing. It wasn't simple jealousy, it was insanity, and she had no way to talk her out of it.

The telephone rang, startling her. She started to go to it, but Brenda cut her off. "No, we need to go now."

"To the airport." Rachael knew she had to stall for time. "I'd better get my suitcase so we can leave." She was hoping Brenda would let her go on her own, but Brenda wasn't that far gone, she followed right behind her with the gun pointed at her back.

"I can get it on my own, it's not heavy," Rachael tried.

"I'll help."

When Rachael paused at the bottom of the stairs, the woman gave her a hard nudge. Moving slowly, it took nearly a full minute to reach the bedroom.

Rachael reached for her bag lying at the head of the bed, but instead of being hurried out, Brenda moved around the room slowly. Lingering by the bed, she ran her fingers over the spread.

"Is this Brand's side?"

"No, he likes the other side."

"Then this will be my side. He will make love to me here."

The very thought made Rachael sick. With the bag in her hand, she edged to the door needing to get out of the room. "We'd better hurry, if I'm going to make my plane."

"Oh," Brenda raised her head. "You're not," she said simply. "They'll think you did, but you won't."

"What do you mean?" Rachael fought to keep her voice from cracking, side-stepping toward the doorway.

"You'll check in with your bag and give your boarding pass to the attendant then while they're distracted, you will slip away." She shrugged her shoulders.

"Why would I do that? I need to go home."

"If you went home, Brand would follow so you'll have to disappear."

"I'm not going to the airport," Rachael stated the obvious, still edging closer to the door.

"I have a wig waiting in the car. No one will suspect that it isn't you who caught the plane. Then I'll come back and take care of you so no one will ever find your body. You see the jealous little bride couldn't take it. So she ran away. Leaving her husband to the woman he should've been with all along."

Rachael was about to make a break for the door when the woman shrieked. "You're pregnant!" She snatched up the prenatal vitamins Rachael hadn't realized she'd forgotten on the dresser.

Fury transformed the woman's face giving Rachael added momentum. She dropped her bag and dove out the door as the gun was raised to fire. The bullet hit the door behind her. Rachael headed for the stairs but knew she wouldn't make it before Brenda's bullet found her back.

Dodging into Dallas' room, she slipped into the walk-in closet. It was set almost like Brand's, but there were more suits and suit coats. Rachael hid behind one of them, grabbing a leather belt from the rack as she did. It wasn't a great weapon, especially against a gun, but it was better than nothing, and she refused to go down without a fight.

Forcing herself to be calm so she could think and listen wasn't easy. She heard the phone ring again, continuing until the answering machine picked it up. Brenda was at the closet door before Rachael heard her. Brenda moved past her hiding place once, but started moving slowly around the closet, pushing clothes aside.

She was only about four feet from her when Rachael knew she had to act. Plowing through the clothes, Rachael hit hard as thunder roared from the gun, echoing in the confines of the closet.

Rachael felt the sting on her side as the bullet passed before hitting the clothes and the wall behind. Not giving Brenda a second chance to fire, she lashed out with the belt. She hit again as the woman staggered back, and then ran, hoping that Brenda wouldn't have time to bring the gun back up.

Brenda was still screaming from the closet when Rachael made it to the stairs. Her momentum down them was too fast, making her stumble on the last couple steps. She caught herself on the railing and swung around the post.

Running through the family room, she paused only long enough to snatch the portable phone. She made out the doors onto the patio. Punching in the emergency number, she slid behind a bush and prayed that the call would go through.

When it was answered, she almost sobbed in relief. "Help me, please. This is Rachael Morgan." She whispered as loudly as she dared. "I'm at the Morgan ranch, and Brenda Blaine is trying to kill me."

"Is this a prank call because if it is, it's punishable—"

Rachael cut the person off. "It's not a prank. She has a gun."

"You said Brenda Blaine," the voice said in disbelief.

"Yes," Rachael cried. "Listen, get someone here to arrest me if you believe I'm lying, just get someone out here. She's already hit me once, and I'm afraid she'll find me. She's insane."

Tears were coming hot down her face. She touched her ribs. They felt like they were on fire, the stickiness of the blood made her stomach roll, and the trembling in her body multiplied though she knew it was only a scratch.

ᑳᑲ

Brand was reaching the main road when his phone rang. "Hello."

"Brand!" He heard Carl, one the sheriff's deputies and a friend on the line. "I just tried to call you at the house. When you didn't answer, I decided to try your cell. Listen, I was here in the area and was going to give John a hand with the stallion."

"I couldn't get a hold of him so I'm on my way," Brand said back.

"Well that's why I'm calling. I've been up and down the road," the deputy came back. "And there's no need, your stallion is in his pasture as peaceful as he can be. There are no horses out of the fence down here anywhere."

"All right, thanks for calling. Wait a minute, you said you called the house and no one answered."

"Yeah."

"But Rachael's there." He punched the disconnect button then the home phone number as he made a U-turn. A bad feeling spread through him as the phone rang unanswered in his ear. He tried to convince himself that Rachael was just getting ready but pressed down hard on the gas pedal. Brand skidded to a stop in front of the house. He leaped from the vehicle not bothering to close the door before running up the walk.

"Rachael," he called bursting through the door. "Rachael, sweetheart," he called again going to the stairs. He stopped as he heard a noise in the family room. "Rachael." He stepped back off the stairs and headed across the hardwood floor, skidding to a stop as the woman moved into the doorway.

"Brenda, what are you doing here?" The wave of uneasiness was stronger than ever.

"I came to do you a favor, but you don't want it, do you? You want her, don't you? You got her pregnant," Brenda snarled.

There was such stress on what she said that Brand's fear jumped to terror. "Where's Rachael?"

"I forgave you for bringing her here." Brenda ignored what he said. "I knew she tricked you into marrying her because you were always supposed to be mine. You weren't supposed to make her pregnant." She brought her hand up with the gun pointing it directly at him.

"Brenda, where's Rachael? What did you do to her?"

Brenda waved her hand. "I took care of your mistake, but you betrayed me. You lied. You want her. You got her pregnant." She shoved the gun out toward his chest. "You shouldn't have touched her. We were to be together."

"It wasn't an accident with the tranquilizer gun. You also shot at her, caused her accident." Brand tried to think of a way to get the gun from her. He had to find Rachael.

"She should have got the message she wasn't wanted here. She should've left."

"You should've told me you wanted us to be together. I didn't know," Brand said stepping forward. "You always had so many men around you."

The gun lowered as he talked.

"I pretended they were you, but they never were. Now, as soon as I kill your mistake, it will be over, then we will be together."

Brand's knees almost collapsed beneath him in relief. She hadn't killed Rachael yet. He wanted to ask where she was but knew that would be disastrous. Trying to still his wild heart, he walked toward the woman he had known all his life but never really knew at all.

"Then you have a plan?" He saw a movement by the patio doors and caught a glimpse of Rachael. Praying she wouldn't misunderstand what was happening, he kept walking forward.

"I–" Brenda started to say when Rachael yelled, cutting her off.

"Brand, careful, she has a gun."

Brenda turned at the same time firing. Brand leapt, taking her down with a flying tackle. Another shot went off shattering a lamp before Brand wrestled the gun away from her. In the middle of the commotion, the front door was shoved open by the deputy with his gun drawn.

"Man, Carl, I'm glad to see you," Brand said, looking over his shoulder while trying to keep hold of the fighting woman.

"We received a call that Brenda was trying to kill your wife." He edged forward as if not really believing his eyes.

"Yeah, do you have a pair of handcuff handy and can you get that gun out of her reach?"

He held on while Carl fastened on the cuffs then released her to him.

"Rachael," Brand called, heading for the patio, leaving the deputy reading Brenda her rights. Rachael peeked around the corner and then she came running toward him and threw herself in his arms. She hugged him tight until he bumped into her scraped ribs. At her pained gasp, he pushed her back.

"You're shot." Seeing the blood on her shirt, he dropped to his knees, pulling at her shirt.

"Brand, stop." She tried to catch his hands. "It's just a scratch."

He refused to give in, pushing the material up. "I want to see." He revealed the place where the skin had been grazed.

"She should have died." Brenda cursed behind them then shrieked when Brand placed a kiss on Rachael's stomach. "No, no, no!" Brenda tried to break free. "You're mine," she screamed as Carl tried to get her out of the house.

Brand stood and scooped Rachael into his arms.

"Brand, I'm okay. It just burns." She tried to soothe him. His worry was palpable.

"Well, I'm not. I need to have you near me." He moved to the sofa and sat with her in his lap. He pressed a row of kisses along her neck and up to her cheek before he caught her mouth. He devoured her hungrily as if he couldn't get enough of her. As if afraid she would be snatched away from him at any minute.

One hand cradled her while the other came up to cup her face, holding her for his kisses then caressing her cheek when he pulled back. "I thought she'd killed you. I thought … I'm so sorry. I didn't know she was like that. Please forgive me."

"I love you," Rachael said, giving him a sweet, gentle kiss.

"I think we're going to miss our plane." He stroked her face.

"It's all right, there's no hurry. We can go later."

"If you can stay out of trouble." He kissed her nose.

"That doesn't seem possible, so you'll just have to keep close track of me." Her kiss was lingering, giving all she had to reaffirm her love for him.

"Umm," he growled. "You can get into all the trouble you want."

It brought back what the nurse had said to her in the hospital. "You're my Brand of trouble." She smiled up.

"Oh," he said with a grin.

"Oh, yes." She kissed him.

About the Author

I grew up in a small town in Wyoming loving the outdoors, sports, art, and reading Hardy Boys books. After reading them all at least a half dozen times, I started writing my own stories.

Thirty years ago I married a wonderful, honorable man. I'm mother of five children and grandmother of six boys. I love traveling. Through my husband's work and vacations, I have visited much of the United States, all over Eastern Europe, Canada, Mexico, China, Thailand, Cambodia and Australia, giving me many intriguing locations and experiences for my stories.

I am a storyteller. I write the classic hero story because I think there's a need for more heroes, love, and adventure in our lives. I'm not out to change the world with my writing; I'm just hoping to make your day a little better.

Hope you enjoy.
Alysia S. Knight

Please feel free to visit me through my website:
www.alysiasknight.com